MW01487953

Her Defender

Protecting Diana Series, Volume 2

Lexy Timms

Published by Dark Shadow Publishing, 2018.

HER DEFENDER

First edition. August 10, 2018.

Written by Lexy Timms.

Also by Lexy Timms

A Chance at Forever Series
Forever Perfect
Forever Desired
Forever Together

BBW Romance Series
Capturing Her Beauty
Pursuing Her Dreams
Tracing Her Curves

Beating the Biker Series
Making Her His
Making the Break
Making of Them

Billionaire Banker Series
Banking on Him

Billionaire Holiday Romance Series
Driving Home for Christmas
The Valentine Getaway
Cruising Love

Billionaire in Disguise Series
Facade
Illusion
Charade

Billionaire Secrets Series
The Secret
Freedom
Courage
Trust
Impulse
Billionaire Secrets Box Set Books #1-3

Building Billions
Building Billions - Part 1
Building Billions - Part 2
Building Billions - Part 3

Conquering Warrior Series

Ruthless

Diamond in the Rough Anthology
Billionaire Rock
Billionaire Rock - part 2

Dominating PA Series
Her Personal Assistant - Part 1
Her Personal Assistant Box Set

Fake Billionaire Series
Faking It
Temporary CEO
Caught in the Act
Never Tell A Lie
Fake Christmas

Firehouse Romance Series
Caught in Flames
Burning With Desire
Craving the Heat
Firehouse Romance Complete Collection

For His Pleasure

Elizabeth

Georgia

Madison

Fortune Riders MC Series

Billionaire Biker

Billionaire Ransom

Billionaire Misery

Fragile Series

Fragile Touch

Fragile Kiss

Fragile Love

Hades' Spawn Motorcycle Club

One You Can't Forget

One That Got Away

One That Came Back

One You Never Leave

One Christmas Night

Hades' Spawn MC Complete Series

Hard Rocked Series

Rhyme

Harmony

Finding Justice
Chasing Justice
Pursuing Justice
Justice - Complete Series

Love You Series
Love Life
Need Love
My Love

Managing the Bosses Series
The Boss
The Boss Too
Who's the Boss Now
Love the Boss
I Do the Boss
Wife to the Boss
Employed by the Boss
Brother to the Boss
Senior Advisor to the Boss
Forever the Boss
Christmas With the Boss
Gift for the Boss - Novella 3.5

Model Mayhem Series
Shameless
Modesty

Moment in Time
Highlander's Bride
Victorian Bride
Modern Day Bride
A Royal Bride
Forever the Bride

Outside the Octagon
Submit

Protecting Diana Series
Her Bodyguard
Her Defender

Reverse Harem Series
Primals
Archaic
Unitary

RIP Series
Track the Ripper
Hunt the Ripper
Pursue the Ripper

Tattooist Series
Confession of a Tattooist
Surrender of a Tattooist
Heart of a Tattooist
Hopes & Dreams of a Tattooist

Tennessee Romance
Whisky Lullaby
Whisky Melody
Whisky Harmony

The Bad Boy Alpha Club
Battle Lines - Part 1
Battle Lines

The Brush Of Love Series
Every Night
Every Day
Every Time
Every Way
Every Touch

The Debt
The Debt: Part 1 - Damn Horse

The Debt: Complete Collection

The University of Gatica Series
The Recruiting Trip
Faster
Higher
Stronger
Dominate
No Rush
University of Gatica - The Complete Series

T.N.T. Series
Troubled Nate Thomas - Part 1
Troubled Nate Thomas - Part 2
Troubled Nate Thomas - Part 3

Undercover Series
Perfect For Me
Perfect For You
Perfect For Us

Unknown Identity Series
Unknown
Unpublished
Unexposed
Unsure

Unwritten
Unknown Identity Box Set: Books #1-3

Unlucky Series
Unlucky in Love
UnWanted
UnLoved Forever

Wet & Wild Series
Stormy Love
Savage Love
Secure Love

Worth It Series
Worth Billions
Worth Every Cent
Worth More Than Money

Standalone
Wash
Loving Charity
Summer Lovin'
Love & College
Billionaire Heart
First Love
Frisky and Fun Romance Box Collection

Managing the Bosses Box Set #1-3

Her
DEFENDER
PROTECTING DIANA SERIES #2
USA TODAY BESTSELLING AUTHOR
LEXY TIMMS

Copyright 2018

1. http://bookcoverbydesign.co.uk/

Protecting Diana Series

Her Bodyguard – Book 1
Her Defender – Book 2
Her Champion – Book 3
Book 4 – coming soon!
Book 5 – coming soon!

Find Lexy Timms:

LEXY TIMMS NEWSLETTER:
http://eepurl.com/9i0vD
Lexy Timms Facebook Page:
https://www.facebook.com/SavingForever
Lexy Timms Website:
http://www.lexytimms.com

Want to read more...
For **FREE**?
Sign up for Lexy Timms' newsletter
And she'll send you updates on new releases, ARC copies of books
and a whole lotta fun!
Sign up for news and updates!
http://eepurl.com/9i0vD

Her Defender Blurb

BY USA TODAY BESTSELLING Author, Lexy Timms.

Ethan Stark's security company is one of—if not—the best. With his Special Forces background, coupled with his family's resources, he's the perfect man for the job. He just wasn't prepared for the politician's daughter with a body that could make grown men weep, and an attitude that puts his teeth on edge.

Ethan has three rules:

Never get personally involved.

Never get blindsided.

And never screw around. Ever.

He's somehow managed to break all three rules and he's got to figured out how to fix the mess he's in. With Diana missing and Ethan's team searching for her, the clock is ticking down.

Except Diana isn't playing the game Ethan thinks she's playing. The threat on the Logans is real—and dangerous. Diana can't seem to get it through her pretty head that this is a game of life and death.

Ethan hauls her off to a safe house, determined to keep this beautiful, infuriating woman out of harms way. But, being cooped up with Diana is more tempting than he thought, and soon Ethan finds himself spiraling into the abyss of Diana's eyes. Of her warm body against his.

All the while, the threat looms. Can Ethan keep her safe? Can he reconcile his feelings for her with a promise he made in his past? Or will the two of them collide like crashing waves and leave nothing but destruction in their wake?

Chapter 1

Ethan

"Anything?" I asked.

"Got nothing on this side of town," Liam said.

"Mason, anything on her credit cards?" I asked.

"Nada. I'm rescanning her father's now, just in case. He says he's got some accounts open in some places. That may be how she's getting around without using her own," Mason said.

"Run and re-run them. She's been gone for almost twenty-four hours. Once we hit that last hour, we have to assume she's been taken," I said.

By now, I was going out of my mind with frustration. I knew that girl hadn't been taken. She was probably prancing around the damn city in her cute little high heels and her shorts, flagging down taxis and paying for them with tit flashes. Damn it to hell, this woman was going to run me into the ground with anger. But even though I knew her better than that, I couldn't stop the layer of fear from creeping up within me.

What if she had been taken?

What if I had lost her?

As I rode around town, keeping my eyes on the sidewalks, my mind began to wander. I still couldn't begin to understand the hold this woman had on me. At first, I wrote it off as carnal. A desire that I hadn't fulfilled in my own body for years. It was nothing but my dick taking control of my mind, and that was that. But as I rolled through the streets of D.C. and communicated with my team, I started wondering if there was something else there.

I shook the thought from my head. There was no way I was going down that path again. I squinted my eyes as I whipped a U-turn in the middle of the road and began heading back in the other direction. I had a task in front of me I needed to complete, and with every minute that slipped by the senator lost faith in my team.

Lost faith in me.

Throughout the past twenty-one hours, I'd been disappointed in the scant information provided by Senator Logan about where his daughter might have disappeared to. It was as if he didn't know anything about his daughter at all. He didn't know her regular hang-out places or where she went shopping. Not even what spa she frequented or where her fucking friends lived. It was as if I had been asking him about the whereabouts of a stranger. Not his own daughter.

It made me look at him in an entirely different light.

He didn't know what Diana did with her spare time, which reinforced the sadness I'd seen in her eyes that day. The sadness of her words. It made me look at the things she had yelled at her father from a different perspective and I could see why she would get so frustrated with him. If he had really been that absent, then his sudden attention towards her would provoke anyone to be upset. Confused. Just having his attention directed at her for once would remind her of the attention she didn't get as a child, throwing more fuel onto the fire.

I began to see all of Diana's anger in a different light.

Including her spoiled brat little attitude.

At the very least, the senator didn't spend time with his daughter. But something deep down told me it was much more than that. After giving it some thought, I logged all of my theories away for when I would need them. Now I came to a stop in between two SUVs and rolled down my windows. Liam to my right, and Mason to my left.

"How's the senator?" I asked Mason.

"Not good. And he still doesn't have any information for us regarding the whereabouts of his daughter," he said.

"Did you find anything in Georgetown?" I asked Liam.

"Not a damn thing. We went back to that party sight, and I've got men canvassing their home. No one's seen her come or go, and no one has any idea who she spends her time with—except that Harper chick the senator mentioned earlier," he said.

"Did you go by her house? See if Diana was there?" I asked.

"Yep. No one was home. At least, there were no cars and no one answered. I walked around the property. Gazed through the windows. I didn't see anything," he said.

"We'll check it later. As far as we know, she doesn't have anyone else in the city," I said.

"Is it possible she left the city?" Mason asked.

"She was pissed about having to leave the city to begin with. I don't think she'd leave it, no," I said.

"How long have we been looking?" Liam asked.

I sighed and pinched the bridge of my nose.

"We're coming up on hour twenty-two," I said.

"Want to start coordinating for a search and rescue team once hour twenty-four hits?" Mason asked.

"We'll figure that out at hour twenty-three," I said.

All of us fell silent as my mind began to swirl.

"Hold on, I'm getting a phone call," Mason asked.

Liam and I whipped our heads over to him as he instantly began typing on his laptop.

"What is it?" I asked.

He held up his finger before his hands began flying across the keyboard.

"Uh huh. And you're sure it was her? Yes, that's perfect. Thank you so much. Would it be possible for you guys to grant me permission to tap into your security cameras?"

He turned his laptop towards us and I saw footage already rolling across his screen.

"No, just permission is fine. I can do it from where I am, but I want footage confirming that it's really Diana. Is that all right?" Mason asked.

My eyes widened when Diana's form came into view on the screen.

"That's her," Liam whispered.

Holy shit. We had footage of Diana still in the city.

"Thank you so much for your cooperation. Once I have the footage downloaded, I'll log out. Mhm. Thank you. You too. Uh huh. Buh-bye," Mason said.

"Permission?" I asked.

"Maybe I moved a little quicker than her mouth did. So what?" he asked, shrugging.

"Where is this?" I asked.

"Violet Boutique, in the heart of downtown D.C. I put out a blast to all of the high-end retail stores in the area that if they saw Diana Logan, to contact my number. That was the front desk woman calling me to let me know that Diana had come in late yesterday and was looking at some clothes before she left without anything," Mason said.

Left without anything? That didn't seem like Diana at all.

"Who's that?" I asked.

"Who's who?" Mason asked.

"Back up the footage. Back it up, Mason."

"All right. All right. I'm going. Damn," he said.

"What is it, Stark?" Liam asked.

"My gut," I said.

Mason backed up the footage and I confirmed that it was Diana. And then a few minutes later, a man in cargo pants and a Hawaiian shirt walked into the store. His head was bald and his stature was tall. Something about him didn't resonate well with me.

"Call them back," I said.

"The store?" Mason asked.

"Yes. Call them back and ask if they remember a man in a Hawaiian shirt," I said.

Mason called back and the second he asked the question, I watched his face fall. Then, he put the call on speakerphone. Liam got out of his car and came around, standing in between the two vehicles so he could better hear the conversation.

"You know what? I do remember him. Bald hair and cargo pants, right?" she asked.

"That's the one. Did he seem out of the ordinary?" Mason asked.

His fingers flew across the keyboard and quickly got me access to the inside of the store. Multiple televisions popped up onto his screen as my eyes panned over each and every one of them.

"Not really. Then again, I had other customers to tend to. But, he didn't come up to me and speak or anything," the woman said.

But my eyes saw what was unfolding on Mason's laptop. He might not have talked to the clerk at the counter, but he had talked with Diana. And by the way she reacted, the interaction wasn't welcomed nor positive.

"Thank you for your time," I said.

"Wait, who is tha—"

Mason hung up the phone and quickly downloaded the footage without my asking. Liam's body pulled taut. A move he mindlessly did when he knew danger was afoot. The three of us watched the man inch closer to her. Pressing her between a wall of clothes and a tall rack of jackets that almost concealed her from us.

"Son of a bitch, he knew where the cameras were," I said.

In a flash, Diana hurried out of the store, and I could see panic written all over her features. Mason worked to get a decent angle of the man's face, but all he could come up with was a three-quarter view of some blurry ass picture.

"I've got it running through my database, but it'll take me time to whittle down who this man is. And that's only if he's got some sort of criminal or military record. If he's clean—"

"Then he's in the wind," I said.

We all raced back to the senator's hotel room and briefed him on what we had found. He seemed relieved that she was at least in the city, but he wasn't impressed that we didn't know who the man was. I wanted to tell him that I wasn't impressed that he didn't know where his daughter would go during a time like this, but I held my tongue. My team and I stayed up all that night trying to track down the identity of the mystery stranger's identity, as well as Diana's possible location. I let Mason and Liam catch some sleep while I kept my eyes on the rolling script on Mason's laptop. They needed to rest.

I, however, couldn't sleep.

The image of the panic on Diana's face had seared itself into my memory. Whatever that man had said or done to her behind that clothing rack had spooked her enough to run out of the store without buying anything. Maybe it had something to do with the threats the Logan family had been receiving. Maybe that man was somehow connected to all this.

I didn't believe in coincidences.

"Ethan! Get over here!" Mason exclaimed.

I dashed into the small kitchen in the senator's hotel room.

"What is it?" I asked.

"I know Diana doesn't have her cell phone on her, but I was able to hack into it. Maybe we can figure out where she is or who she might be with from the contents of her phone," Mason said.

"Perfect. What do you have?" I asked.

"For one, the sheer number of men she's texting with."

"How long as she been texting them?"

I bit down on my tongue to keep myself from digging a deeper hole as Mason shot me a weird look.

"Uh—varying amounts of time, it looks like. Some for months, others for days. But none of them in the past week or so. At least, she hasn't been texting them. Though they sure as hell have been texting her."

We flipped through her text messages and the sheer amount of dick pictures and scantily clad torsos that littered her inbox made me sick. But it was all we had. Since she wasn't using her credit cards or drawing money out of her checking account, she had either left town after than man spooked her or she was staying with someone she knew. I didn't think she was foolish enough to leave the D.C. area. Even after being spooked so badly.

"Look for clues as to someone she could be in the city with. A close friend. A relative. A trusted confidant," I said.

"I'm surfing through things right now, but honestly? I'm still in the photos," Mason said.

The more pictures we soared through, the sicker I became. Just another difference between her and Layla. Diana was a party girl. Miss Popular with the boys. A millennial who strived for likes on her Instagram account rather than the likes of people who interacted with her on a daily basis. Then again, with the death of her mother and the rift between her and her father, seeking attention like that shouldn't have shocked me. But even so, she wasn't the type of girl to settle down. It looked as if she kept men in a little black book on her cell phone for whenever she got lonely.

A man-eater. That's apparently what Diana was. And I had to keep reminding myself of that every time I saw our indiscretion in a gentler light. I was nothing but a notch on her post. Another man she had conquered before chewing me up and spitting me out.

Layla hadn't been any of that.

"I've got something," Mason said.

"What is it?" I asked.

"There are actually two addresses stored for Harper Riley in Diana's phone. Liam checked one, but he didn't know about the other," Mason said.

He sent the address to my phone and I looked over at Liam.

"Ready to go get her?" I asked.

"Yep," Liam said.

"Mason, you stay here and keep digging through that phone. I want all the information I can get on her before we turn it back over to her. And right now, I'm not so sure we even will," I said.

"She's going to hate you for that," Mason said, chuckling.

"Well, I hate her for a lot of things right now, so we'll break even and keep going. Chastain? Come on. We have a spoiled little child to go get," I said.

"If I didn't know any better, I'd say you were ready to paddle that behind of hers."

I stopped at the door frame and shot him a glaring look as my anger mounted.

But he was right. If Diana threw up any sort of a fight, I had no idea what I was going to do with her, short of tossing her over my shoulder and throwing her into the SUV.

Chapter 2

Diana

With a sigh, I turned off the sixty-inch flat screen television. I tossed the remote onto the side table before I sat up on the couch. Harper's place was boring as hell, especially when she didn't want to get up before noon. I'd raced to the house her parents rented out for her in Georgetown after my little encounter with the weirdo in the clothing shop and she took me right in. We stayed up all night drinking and laughing. Gossiping about boys and the latest parties that had gone up in flames because we weren't there. I indulged her with stories, like how my father was losing his fucking mind and how the only thing that made it bearable was Ethan's hunky little ass.

I didn't tell her about our encounter, though. I wanted to make her drool first.

Whenever I got drunk and passed out, I was an early riser. Harper, on the other hand, was not. It was already eleven thirty and I could still hear her snoring. The worst part was that every time my mind went blank, it rushed back to the encounter I'd had with that man in the shop.

The fact that he knew my name set me on edge. Then the fact that he kept rattling on about whether or not I was 'ready' creeped me out. But when he said he was curious as to why I had slipped my father's protection detail, I was actually frightened. He alluded to a dangerous world, and who was taking care of me now. It was enough to get me to drop the clothes in my arms and leave the store, then I quickly hailed a cab and headed straight for Harper's house.

Her place was somewhere I could hide out and get my bearings without encountering her parents. This house that Harper had moved into a couple of years ago had been a present from her parents. She had gone to community college and gotten an associate's degree in cosmetology or something like that and they rewarded her with her own damn rented home.

I on the other hand, graduated with a Bachelor's in Business, and all my father rewarded me with was a blank stare and an empty seat at graduation.

Sighing, I began walking around the house. I knew this was somewhere I could hide until I figured out my next move. She wouldn't toss me out on my ass, no matter how many times she'd tossed me under the bus. Harper's house had four guest bedrooms, and two of them were on the opposite end of the house. We didn't even have to see one another if we didn't want to.

While Harper had listened to me drone on about my situation last night, there were times when she had rolled her eyes. She had scoffed, and done things that made me feel as if she didn't believe me, or didn't care about my predicament. Some part of me wondered if Harper thought I was making all this up just to get attention. There were times where she certainly looked at me as if I was. All eyes, and gazing up and down my body with her nose wrinkled.

Whatever.

She didn't have to believe me if she didn't want to.

Harper had wanted to go out to the club last night, but I faked a headache and stayed in. I'd had enough to drink and was ready to slide into bed anyway, despite Harper teasing me about acting like an old broad. I had made one of Harper's guest bedrooms my own and flopped down into bed with alcohol coursing through my veins. But once Harper had left the house after listening to me talk for damn near three hours, my mind drifted back to Ethan.

To his men in the shoe store.

I'd fallen asleep with regret on my mind last night. The alcohol had lowered my inhibitions enough to feel bad for giving them the slip. I'd been so mad at Ethan and felt so rejected after experiencing such happiness in his arms that I didn't know any other way to make him hurt the way he had hurt me. Happiness followed by the rejection wasn't something I'd ever dealt with well. I didn't enjoy the feeling of being tossed to the side like he had done with me. And now I'd made it all worse by acting out because of that hurt. An immature reaction that had tossed me into a very dangerous situation.

The more I thought about it, the more I began to believe that maybe my family had come under siege after all

What I had done was dangerous, and with that man approaching me in that store, the threat against my family now seemed more serious than I had originally believed. Something in my gut told me he was connected to all of this, the bald man with the Hawaiian shirt. But Ethan had been such a jerk after we had made love that I couldn't help myself. There was no way I was going to stick around and let him act like nothing happened between us when we had shared something so personal. Something that connected and bonded us. I'd never let a man cum inside me like that. I always made them wear protection despite being on birth control. But I wanted that connection with Ethan. I wanted that closeness. I wanted his mark inside of my body.

He should be thankful I had deigned to rock his world instead of acting like he was my dirty little secret.

Finding myself in the kitchen, I grabbed an apple from the fruit bowl on the kitchen island. My mind fell back to the man in the store. Who was he? What was his role in all this? He obviously knew who I was and he knew the situation I'd been in. Was he watching me? Tracking me? I found myself getting paranoid in front of all the kitchen windows, so I made my way back to the bedroom I was using. I closed the blinds as I held the apple between my teeth, then I sat on the edge of the bed.

I felt ridiculous, but my gut wouldn't stop screaming at me.

Why had that man let me walk away from him if I was a target? Was he only trying to scare me and my father? Or was it part of some kind of cat and mouse game he was playing with us? I didn't like it. Someone was playing with us—a game I didn't do well with. Was that man building up to some final act?

Maybe an act that would result in our deaths?

I shivered as I slowly ate my apple. I really hoped I was wrong and that it was only my mind getting carried away with me again. But sitting in the dark room with the shades pulled and no way to protect myself, I suddenly wished Ethan was there with me. Sitting in the corner, ready to protect me at a moment's notice. Even though I couldn't stand him, and though he had hurt me in ways I wasn't ready to acknowledge yet, I understood how vulnerable I was without him. I knew he would protect me, despite the hatred and disgust he apparently felt towards me.

The bedroom door flying open caught my attention and ripped me from my trance. I let out a scream of terror as I jumped up from the bed, ripping the apple from my mouth and holding it over my head. My screaming was met with the familiar screams of another person before her voice filled the air.

"What the fuck is wrong with you!?" Harper exclaimed.

She turned on the light and saw me standing there with my apple poised over my head. She looked at me with a dubious stare before she went back to rubbing the sleep out of her makeup-caked eyes. I brought the apple down and placed it on the empty dresser as my eyes panned over to the clock on the bedside table. It was still only a quarter to noon. What was Harper doing awake?

"Have a bad dream?" I asked.

"No. Got guests," Harper murmured.

Then, I heard heavy footsteps sounding down the hallway.

I watched Ethan push past my friend and stride right into the room. My heart pounded in my chest. I knew I would be found eventually. I knew he would come for me and try to take me back. But I hadn't prepared myself for what to do when he did find me. When I did see him for the first time since I'd given his men the slip. Mr. Man Bun stood in the doorway with a very angry look on his face. His arms were crossed over his chest as Ethan came and practically pinned my ass to the dresser. He glared at me with eyes that spilled an unrelenting anger into my face and I felt my mouth go dry as his body heat pounded against me.

Shit.

Even in his anger, I wanted him more than I could stand.

Chapter 3

Ethan

Staring down at Diana, my chest swelled with my deep breaths. Inside, I was relieved. I was staring into the eyes of a Diana that was still alive—instead of looking at her dead, mangled body in an alleyway. But the relief I'd felt the second her friend told me she was there was quickly overwhelmed by my anger towards her. The second I barreled through the room and laid eyes on her, my body began to tremble with frustration. My hands stayed fisted at my sides as Liam quickly worked Diana's friend, Harper, out of the bedroom. Then he guarded the doorway in case she tried to run, and I stood there, pinning her between the dresser and the anger of my stare.

"Pack your things," I said.

"I don't have any things except my purse," Diana said.

"Grab it then, we're leaving."

I watched her nod before she wiggled out from underneath me and my brow furrowed. My eyes panned over towards her and I watched her gather her purse, putting the few things she had sprawled out on the bedside table back inside. Without any sass and without any argument, she closed her purse and stood there. Her eyes connected with mine as I heard Liam grunt, and I whipped my head over and found Harper approaching Diana's side.

I eyed Liam heavily before he shrugged his shoulders.

We were going to have to have a very serious conversation when we got back to the hotel room.

"You didn't mention how hot your security squad was," Harper said.

But Diana's eyes never wavered from mine.

"Can you hook a sister up?" Harper asked.

And still, Diana didn't waver.

"I'm ready when you guys are," she said.

I narrowed my eyes at her before she walked past her friend, not answering her little question. Confusion littered Liam's features as he backed out of the room and began escorting Diana down the hallway. She walked out of that room with pride. With strength. With her head held high, and without engaging her obviously immature friend. I felt Harper's eyes on me as I left the room. She was probably staring at my ass or something. It shouldn't have shocked me that Diana's best friend would act just like she did.

What shocked me was Diana's immediate compliance with my demand.

I followed behind Liam and Diana, holding back my need to chastise her. But only barely. The words were right there on the tip of my tongue, ready to be fired off the second she back-talked. Or broke down. Or threw one of her little fits. But she did none of that. As we maneuvered through the house until we got to the front door, I watched Diana reach out for the doorknob.

And in an instant, I reached out for her and ripped her back.

"What's wrong?" Diana asked.

She stumbled next to me before I motioned for Liam to open the door.

"Check the perimeter before we take her to the car," I said.

The rush of electricity as my hand clamped down around her arm shot my body into overdrive. My anger quickly faded away and the relief at having her near me again filled my body. The veins in my groin pulsed. Electricity stood up the hairs on the back of my neck. I wanted to draw her into my arms and kiss her. To hug her, and chastise her for running away before chanting how thankful I was that she was alive. That she was safe and well.

But I pushed all of that down into my gut. Down into a place I never wanted to touch again. I needed to be cold. Detached. Aware of my surroundings.

I didn't need Diana dimming my attention to this case.

"We're good," Liam said.

"Let's go," I said.

And to my utter shock, she obeyed without a second thought.

I escorted her out to the SUV and put her in the passenger's seat. Closing the door, I wrapped around to the driver's side, then came face-to-face with Liam. The two of us needed to have a bit of a talk, and I wasn't going another step without having it.

"I know I told you not to put your hands on women, but surely you know I meant that in a sexual way. Why the hell did Harper make it back into that room?" I asked.

"She shoved past me, Ethan," he said.

"I don't care if she pointed a gun at you. Take it from her, then grab her arm and keep her out in the hallway."

"You know I have a line when it comes to—"

"I don't care what that line is, Liam. You know I'd never ask you to hurt a woman. Ever. You know me better than that. I see you grimace at me when I yank Diana around, but it's to get her to listen. If Harper pushed past you, I would have expected you to reach out, grab her arm, and make her follow your demands. You told her to stay in that hallway, and she should have listened. I told you to keep an eye on Diana, and you should have had her on a fucking leash, Chastain. You should have been sitting right by her with your hand wrapped around her arm."

"Ethan, come on, man."

"If you don't have what it takes to deal with a strong-willed woman who doesn't want to listen, then I'll find someone who does. I get it. The line you have is very understandable. But we're dealing with a bunch of spoiled little children who think they can push and shove and get their way simply by demanding it. Don't like it? That's fine. I don't either. But if you give one of them a command and they don't follow it? Treat them like you would a man who gave you the same disrespect on a case," I said.

"Got it," he said.

"Now, you're heading back to Senator Logan's hotel room. I'm going to be driving Diana to the safe house after loading a couple of our men on a plane—including Mason—to fly her shit to the safe house. Got it?"

"Loud and clear."

"Good. Now get Diana's suitcase out of your car and put it in mine, then get in your car and get to Senator Logan."

Then, I motioned for him to get in his damn car so I could get into mine.

I watched as Liam lugged all of Diana's luggage into my car, then the two of us parted ways. I would make sure her things and my crew got off the ground and headed to the safe house. I started up the vehicle and backed out of Harper's driveway, then headed straight for the tarmac.

And the entire ride over there, the silence was thick and awkward.

"Where are we going?" Diana asked.

I knew it wouldn't be quiet the second she realized we weren't going to her home. Or to the hotel. I debated not answering, but she was in such a compliant mood that I didn't want to chance ruining it with my own stubbornness.

"The safe house," I said.

"Ethan, I'm not going to some dingy cabin in—"

I slammed on my breaks at a red light as my hands curled tightly around the steering wheel.

"I want you to listen and listen good, Diana. You don't have a say in this situation. You don't get to direct or take charge of the demands I make of you. Got it? You haven't been taking this threat seriously, and that's on you. That little stunt you pulled with my men? You could have been hurt. Or killed. You don't have to understand that. I doubt you ever will. But you will understand this. You're going to that safe house where I can keep an eye on you, and it doesn't matter what you have to say about it."

She frowned, then someone honked their horn at me and I turned my attention back towards the road. I watched her face flush as she sank into her seat, but out of the corner of my eye I saw her bite back whatever it was she wanted to say. Another gesture that was greatly unlike her. I furrowed my brow deeper as I wove through D.C., making my way closer to the tarmac. Thank fuck I had a business plane on standby for shit like this.

Driving her to the safe house was going to be a task in and of itself, but the last thing I needed was to add more suitcases and men to that equation.

"I'm sorry," Diana said.

Confused, my eyes flickered over to her as I heard her draw in a deep breath.

"What?" I asked.

"I'm sorry. You know, for ditching the security detail. But I do understand that the threat is real now and that this isn't just my father making up something for the cameras. So, I promise to behave and do what you say, okay?"

"Nice to hear."

"Just please take me home, Ethan."

"No way."

"Don't put me in the woods in a place I'm not familiar with. I'm begging you not to do it."

The pleading in her voice was scratching at my walls, but I couldn't let her crumble them. This was for her own good, whether she would accept that or not.

"You're going to the safe house and that is final. If what you're telling me is true about believing the threat is real, then you understand why I'm doing it," I said.

"Just take me home, Ethan. Please," she said breathlessly.

I looked over at her and saw tears welling in her eyes and it shook me to my core. Her eyes were red. They were getting puffy. Those were real tears. Real tears that signaled real anxiety and real fear coursing through her veins.

With no access to words to answer her, instead, I just shook my head.

"Fucking pathetic little boy," she murmured.

I allowed her curse to roll of my back as we pulled onto the tarmac of the airport. I knew she was scared and upset, but that didn't change anything. My responsibility was to keep her safe and figure out what the hell was going on with her and Senator Logan. If I had to go with her down to the safe house to make sure she didn't pull the wool over my men's eyes again, then so be it. If that is what it took to keep Diana safe, then I would do it. I'd pull my hair out doing it. I'd bite back more anger and sexual frustration than I ever had in my life doing it. But I'd do it.

For her.

"At least the plane is nice," Diana said.

"It's my company plane," I said.

"You have a company plane?"

"I do. For instances like this, actually."

"Where you're flying random women off to your cabin in the woods to coop them up and drive them insane?"

"Or when I'm flying random men off to do the same thing."

I didn't expect her to giggle at my statement, but she did. I whipped my head over to look at her as a small grin crossed her cheeks. And for a second, I pretended she wasn't upset with me. That nothing had happened between us to make her angry with me. I pretended the two of us were okay. That maybe we were taking a trip together after sharing a vulnerable moment that opened us up to a world of romance.

After allowing myself a split second to dream, I ripped myself back to reality.

"So, where do you want me?" Diana asked.

"Stay in the car. We're loading up your things, then hitting the road," I said.

"Wait, hitting the road? We're not flying there?"

I turned off the car and took the keys with me before I engaged the child locks on all the doors. I grinned as I made my way out of my seat and turned to close the door behind me. I slammed my door shut before I unlocked the trunk, then directed my men to unload her things and get them onto the plane.

"You're not even going to leave me some cold air running?" she asked.

"Should have thought about that before you took off," I said.

I grinned as I made my way to the trunk. She tried to unlock her door, her fist banging on the glass. I had a lockdown mode in all my SUVs for situations like this. For unruly clients or men I captured or anything that required a temporary space to lock them in. I walked around to the trunk while she banged against the window, yelling at me to come back. I wasn't going to keep her in there without any air. I wasn't a sadist. But, listening to her finally unravel and curse my name gave me a bit of a thrill. I grinned as I opened the trunk and helped my men pull out her things. Then they took the suitcases and started for the plane. The only other person missing was Mason, and I knew he would only be a few minutes behind me. Diana and I, however, needed to get on the road if we were going to make it to the safe house by sunset.

Next, I hit the button on my key fob and watched as Diana's door flew open.

I heard her grunt as she went falling to the cement, her sandals clacking and her lips cursing my existence. Closing the trunk, I made my way around to Diana's side, watching as she got up off the ground. She dusted herself off before she stretched her limbs, which she needed to more than she knew. Because once we got back into that car, we weren't stopping until I needed gas.

"I think you like seeing me in pain."

Diana's voice hit my ears and my eyes turned to her face. I reached out to try and help her get back into the car, but she ripped her arm away from my touch. Glaring at me, she stood to her full height, tall and prouder than ever. And when my eyes caught hers, my stomach sank.

She wasn't trying to insult me. She was telling the truth. She really thought I enjoyed seeing her in pain, and the realization slapped me across the face.

All the more reason for me to keep my distance until this was all said and done.

"Come on. We have a road trip to take," I said.

Then, I opened her door and ushered her back into her seat as curses against my very existence continued to fall from her lips.

Chapter 4

Diana

Unhappy was an understatement when I learned that I really was being shipped off to some shitty shack in Virginia without my permission. The only thing that made it even partially bearable was the fact that Ethan was coming along this time. I was trying to be nice. Trying to be sweet and not let my personal feelings towards any of this shit get in the way. I got pissed off at myself when I showed him my own fear. Showing him my vulnerability when it came to being back in the woods somewhere was a mistake. But I hated the woods. I hated how dark it was. I hated the quiet and the sounds of the animals moving around in the distance, not to mention trees that could tumble on top of me at any second. I hated every bit of it.

I tried to play nice with Ethan, remembering how well he responded to me acting sweet and vulnerable. But this time, he didn't seem to be falling for it.

Watching the beautiful plane sitting there behind as we drove away made me sick. That plane that would have made this trip much more bearable. It looked nice, and surely had nice food. Maybe even some nice drinks. A nice leather seat for me to sink into. But no, I was cooped up in some stupid ass SUV with a man that practically found humor in the pain he caused me.

"If anything, you're the kidnapper," I murmured.

"If that's how you feel, then that's fine. It won't stop me from keeping you safe," Ethan said.

"Take me home," I said.

"No."

"Now."

"Nope."

"Damn it, Ethan. You take me home now or I'll fight you. I'll punch you right in the jaw, run this damn vehicle off the road, and find a way to escape. Just like I did your men. And you know I'll do it. You know I'm capable of it."

We came to a stop at a red light and he slowly panned his gaze over to mine. The menacing look he had on his face caused me to hold my breath. Laughter fell from his lips, but it wasn't the kind of laughter that made me happy. It wasn't the kind of laughter that was inviting. Or beautiful. Or sexy. Or lewd.

It was cruel.

And as I looked into Ethan's eyes, he didn't care about the cruelty that fell from his lips.

"If you think you can get your way by pretending to be good, then you can go right back to being bad. You can fight all you want, Diana. But I was hired to do a job by your father, and I intend on seeing it through. You're not being kidnapped. Not by me, and not by anyone else. And when this week's congressional hearings are done, your father will be joining us, along with the rest of my men assigned to this case. That is what's best for you, which means you should stop acting like a petulant toddler and accept it."

Without thinking, I rolled down the window and reached outside the door and opened it, then reached for my seatbelt. I got it off me quickly enough to take a step out of the car, but I felt something hard and commanding wrap around my arm. Suddenly, I was pulled off my feet and back into the car before Ethan started pulling forward. I cried out as he slammed on the brakes, shutting the door against my feet. I heard something thud before he released my arm, then we continued our progression forward through the stoplight.

I shoved Ethan in his seat, my fists beating down on his meaty arm.

"Let me out of this bullshit excuse for a car, you asshole!" I exclaimed.

But his face was nothing but a mask of rage.

I sat down in my seat and tried rolling the window down again, but it was no use. I wiggled the door handle, furiously tugging on it before I pounded my foot into the door. I wanted out. I wanted to be done. I wasn't being shoved off to Virginia with yet another man that didn't give a shit about me. At least the damn kidnapper would give a shit about me. Hell, the man was stalking me.

That's way more than my father. I have to start a fight just to get him to say my fucking name!

Ethan's smug attitude grated on my nerves as I wore myself out. Sweat broke out on my brow as we traveled down the road, taking the highway out of D.C. Out of my hometown. Out of the only place I'd ever known. Panic filled my veins and my eyes darted around. My hands were planted on the dashboard of the car as my head panned back and forth. I didn't recognize where we were. I didn't recognize the expanse of the road. My knees felt weak and I couldn't catch my breath and my vision was beginning to tunnel.

Was I dying?

Was this what it felt like to die?

"Diana, sit back."

I felt Ethan's hand press against my stomach as my body fell back to the leather seats of his SUV.

"Diana, look at me."

Tears crested my eyes as my hands grasped the edge of the seat underneath me.

"Diana, can you hear me?"

My eyes looked out the window as my breath came in ragged pants. I couldn't say anything. I couldn't respond. I couldn't do anything other than panic. Why was I panicking? What was happening to my body? I felt like I was going to pass out. I felt unbalanced. Unhinged. Like everything was spiraling out of control and I recognized nothing. Not the roads. Not the signs. Not the sights. Not the sounds. I didn't recognize the man sitting next to me even though I thought I knew him, and I didn't recognize my own life. I stared at my reflection. At the scared little girl with tears streaming down her face.

Tears she shed the day her mother died.

"I want to go home. I want to go home. I want to go home."

I needed to calm down. I needed to let Ethan do his job. The rational part of me understood that. But the farther away we got from D.C., the farther away we got from home. From my mother. From her grave. From her memories and her scent and the perfume of hers I still kept stashed in my vanity.

"I didn't pack it. Oh no, I didn't pack it."

"Didn't pack what, Diana?"

I heard the concern in Ethan's voice, but he still didn't stop the car.

"We have to go back for it. I didn't pack it, Ethan."

"We'll get it when all of this is done. I promise."

"Your promises mean nothing!"

The roar of my voice filled the cabin of the car before I felt myself grow light-headed. I hated Ethan's attitude. I hated how he could sound so disgusting one minute and so sweet the next. His attitude made me sick. It made me angry and frustrated. He was just like my father. Ignoring my wishes and not even trying to understand why I had them in the first damn place. He didn't care about my panic. About my state of mind. About my fears or my sadness or my heartache. Ethan would do whatever he wanted with me, not caring about the effect it had on my life.

Just like my fucking father.

"Listen to me. You're having a panic attack, Diana. I need you to sit up and take deep breaths," Ethan said.

Sitting back in the seat, I straightened myself out, but I still felt out of control. My mother's grave was behind us. Her perfume was behind us. Her clothes were back at the house and the bed she used to sleep in whenever she got sick wasn't in Virginia. I couldn't curl up into the sheets of her own spare bedroom and pretend she was there. I couldn't spritz the last of her handmade perfume onto my clothing and fall asleep in it. None of that was in Virginia.

None of that was in the middle of the damn woods.

I felt Ethan's hand come down on my thigh, but I ripped myself away. I pressed myself against the window and settled my forehead into it. Not even a panic attack stopped him. Not even my pain stopped him. Tears dripped down my cheeks as I finally got control of my mind. Control of my body. Control of my breaths. I watched the city slowly pass by me before the forest gave way to farmland. Cows and horses and goats. Pigs and the disgusting smell of manure.

Great. I was in a place where the livestock outnumbered the people. I was going to be stuck out in the sticks with nothing to do but count the mosquito bites that would eventually riddle my arms. I closed my eyes and imagined a run-down, shoddy little shack. With no electricity and no running water. Survivor-type shit, with nothing but a fire and some damn deer to gnaw on while we passed the time.

Was this something they could use at Guantanamo? Because it sure felt like it.

Relaxing against the window, I allowed my eyes to fall shut, but the second the car stopped they popped open. I gazed out at the truck stop we had pulled into and I heard Ethan's door open. I whipped my head over and watched him get out, but he quickly locked the doors and windows before he shut the door. He walked over to the side and began pumping gas into the SUV we rode in, then he hopped back in and pulled the car into a parking spot in front of the building.

"What are we doing?" I asked.

"Your voice sounds more stable," he said.

"Like you care."

His eyes flickered over to me before he shook his head.

"Follow me inside," he said.

"Why are we going inside?"

"You struggled yourself into a panic attack to get out of the car, and now you're questioning why I'm asking you to get out of the car?"

I bit down onto the inside of my cheek to keep from spiraling into a fit of rage. What an idiot. I didn't panic because I was in a damn car.

It just went to show how little he knew me and how he didn't care about knowing more. And, how stupid I had been to let him get so close.

"Fine. Whatever," I said.

"Thank you," Ethan said.

I followed him into the truck stop and he led us into a shoddy little restaurant. They had rickety chairs with wobbling tables and vinyl-covered booths that had holes in them. I grimaced at the crumbs on the table as Ethan flopped himself down. He groaned as if he had been on his feet for the past ten days straight, relaxing into the pathetic excuse for cushions like they were somehow his savior. I frowned as I sat down onto the edge of the seat. I slowly scooted myself in, trying not to think about the thousands of sweaty asses that had been in this exact spot. An apathetic waitress came over to us with two glasses of water and two stained menus, then dropped it all down in front of us and left.

"Thanks. I'll have a lemonade. Sure," I said.

"Order whatever you want. It's on me," Ethan said.

"What a gentleman," I said flatly.

He peered at me from over his menu, but I paid him no mind. I was too focused on the disgusting menu in front of me. Everything sounded disgusting. Nothing but carb-heavy, gravy-coated monstrosities. Country-fried steak with brown gravy and mashed potatoes. Steak niblets covered in red gravy with beans and rice. Fried chicken with sweet corn and french fries.

Hadn't these people ever heard of a salad?

"Ready to order?" the waitress asked.

"Could I get a lemonade with my water?" I asked.

"We're out," the woman said flatly.

"Do you have anything else to drink?" I asked.

"Sweet tea."

"Anything with a fresh fruit in it?" I asked.

She stared at me blankly as Ethan cleared his throat

"I'll have your double-fried chicken with a slice of your sweet corn-bread, hushpuppies, and some of that honey butter sauce to dip it in."

"Dessert?" the woman asked.

"Banana pudding," Ethan said.

Then, she panned her gaze over to me.

"I guess I shouldn't ask if anything is organic or sustainably-sourced or cruelty-free, huh?" I asked.

"No. You shouldn't," the waitress said.

"I'll have a salad without any cheese," I said.

"Dressing?" the woman asked.

"Oil and vinegar?"

"We got balsamic."

"Sure. I'll take that."

"Anything else to drink?"

"I'm okay with water, but if you have coffee I'd love some," Ethan said.

"Sure thing, sweet cheeks. Anything else?" she asked.

"I'll take a coffee as well," I said.

"I should probably mention it's not organic," the woman said.

Ethan snickered and I felt frustration grow in the pit of my stomach.

"As long as it's made in your kitchen, I'll consider that locally sourced. A cup of coffee would be nice," I said.

"Cream and sugar?" she asked.

"Yes," I said.

"No," Ethan said.

"All right. I'll get your orders in and be back shortly with your local coffees."

The woman tossed a smirk over to Ethan and I chose to ignore it. If they wanted to make fun of me, that was fine. I could handle it. But if this menu and this treatment was a prelude to what the safe house would be like, then I was fucked.

Royally and absolutely fucked.

Chapter 5

Ethan

I figured after driving for a couple of hours it had been time to grab some lunch before we got back onto the road. We had to stop for gas, anyway and my stomach was growling. My place in Abington was still a two-hour drive away and there wouldn't be many places to stop in between. I figured Diana wouldn't take kindly without a professional chef ready to cook for her the instant we walked into the house. Plus, part of me needed a change of scenery from the tension-laden SUV. Diana had completely thrown herself into a panic before winding down and falling asleep, which worried me. I'd never had such a difficult time reading someone before, and just when I finally came to understand what her real tears looked like, she pulled a trick like this out of her hat.

I had no idea why she had panicked, and that really bothered me.

Either way, both of us could use the change of scenery. Especially after I lost my temper on our drive out of the city. I regretted speaking to her so roughly, but it was as if she didn't respond to anything else. It was insane, and I hated every second of it. Why couldn't she just listen? Why did everything have to be such a battle with her?

Then again, she did try to escape from me back in D.C. I shook my head at the thought. Rolling down her window and opening the door from the outside? She was quickly learning how my car worked. But I had more gadgets and gizmos installed on the thing than she could ever dream of. If I wanted to lock her in, she'd stay locked in. But I don't know why she made me resort to that kind of thing in the first place. The girl was hot one minute and cold the next. Why couldn't she simply behave like an adult? Why did she always have to revert to her childish behavior and pitch a bullshit tantrum all the time?

Just because I had my nose was turned up where she was concerned didn't mean my body was immune to her, however. As we sat across from one another in the booth at the little diner, I thought about the relief I had experienced when I first laid eyes on her in Harper's home. And the ecstatic feeling that rushed through my veins when I felt her body heat radiating against mine. It meant her heart was beating, and that life pulsed through her veins. I thought something horrendous had happened to her, and when I found her alive and well at her friend's house I could have kissed her I was so happy to see her.

Every possible scenario had run through my head during the twenty-four hours we tried to find her. I'd imagined every kidnapping scenario. Every torture someone could pull on her. Every trick in the book used to garner whatever information someone thought she had. And the longer the minutes ticked on, the worse my thoughts became. I had convinced myself we'd find her dead. Chopped up in an alley somewhere or tossed into a trash bin after being mangled beyond recognition.

And then, I found her standing in her friend's house.

I'd wanted to pull her into my arms and not let go. I'd wanted to kiss the top of her head and whisper my chastisement, telling her why she shouldn't have done what she did. I wanted to scoop her into my arms and walk her back out to the car, then whisk her away to wherever she wanted to go. Anywhere with me so I could keep her safe.

But that would have been foolish.

Diana wasn't into me. She was simply looking for a distraction from all this drama and fear. And when the case was wrapped up, I wouldn't mean any more to her than any other random guy she texted on her phone. The connection we felt in the garden together? It was probably fabricated. At the very least, she didn't share it. Diana wasn't capable of it. She was a man-eater, judging by the sheer volume of men that pandered for her attention on her phone. She was too selfish to think about anyone but herself. It didn't matter the pain she was in. If that pain manifested as pure selfishness, then a person would stop at nothing to mow down what was in front of them in order to feel validated. In order to feel worth something.

She seduced me to feel worth something, and I gave into that seduction.

A mistake I wouldn't make again.

I was disappointed in myself, yes. But at least I understood the game she was playing now. I had learned her tricks and her tells, meaning I'd be able to read her more closely from now on. Shutting myself down and turning off those feelings before I did something stupid again was critical. That way I'd be able to get myself out of a situation before it escalated into something I wouldn't be able to control.

"A salad with no cheese for you, and fried chicken with cornbread and hushpuppies for you," the waitress said.

"You didn't bring him his honey butter," Diana said.

"Good thing I'm going back to get it then, huh?" the waitress asked.

"And while you're back there, can you see if you guys have any sparkling water?"

"I can tell you for a fact that we don't."

My eyes locked onto Diana's face as she scoffed and shook her head. The waitress walked off to get my honey butter dip and I narrowed my eyes at her. Odd, for her to even care about what the waitress did or didn't bring me.

"Next time we stop, try to find a place that knows what a vegetable is," Diana said.

"We're in the country. Get used to it," I said.

"I won't be gaining weight or putting my health at risk because you wanted to rip me from my home without my permission. You want me at this little house? Then you better tailor it to all of my health needs. Not just keeping me alive."

Her eyes flashed at me and a raw, unadulterated frustration coursed behind them.

"Here's your honey butter, sweetheart. Can I get you guys anything else?" the waitress asked.

"We're good. Thanks," I said.

"Do you have any lettuce back there that isn't wilted?" Diana asked.

I groaned as she picked at her salad with her fork.

"We're fine. Thank you," I said.

Diana scoffed as the waitress shot her a look and walked away. I watched disgust roll over her features as she picked at her salad. And every time she lifted a piece of lettuce to see what was underneath it, her disgust grew.

"You really need to eat something," I said.

"Not this," she said, as she pushed her plate away.

"We aren't stopping for another thing until we get to the safe house. And there isn't a paid chef to cook for you there."

"Is there fresh fruit I can bite into? Because it'll be better than this swill."

"Just eat the damn salad, Diana."

She glared at me before she inched the salad farther away from her. Holy fuck, why did everything have to be such a battle with her? I felt frustration welling in my veins again as she grabbed her coffee and sipped on it. She crinkled her nose, like the coffee wasn't good enough for her either, and I felt something inside me pop. I didn't know why she got under my skin so easily, but if she thought that spoiled attitude would fly while I was around, she had another thing coming.

"What were you thinking when you ditched your security detail?" I asked.

"You mean the little stunt at the shoe shop?" she asked.

She fluttered her eyes over to me and I drew in a deep breath.

"Yes. When you slipped them without notifying anyone of where you were going," I said.

"It's not like notifying them would have done any good. You guys don't let me go anywhere or do anything. I wanted some time to myself and to not be surrounded by your idiotic goons. Duh."

"You know they could have protected you from that man in the clothing store, right?" I asked.

Her face stiffened and her eyes locked hard with mine.

"What did you say?" she asked.

"The man in the Hawaiian shirt. The one that followed you into the store. If my guys had been there, they could have protected you from him."

"How do you know about that?"

"I know about everything, Diana. It's my job."

I watched her look away before she bit down onto her lower lip. She curled her coffee mug close to her body and her entire nonverbal language screamed fear. She had obviously been spooked by the man and still was. I wanted to know what he had said to her. I needed to know. If I was going to keep her and her father safe, I needed to be working with all of the facts.

"Diana."

"What?" she asked.

"Look at me."

"I'm good, thanks."

I sighed and shook my head before I cleared my throat.

"Look at me. I mean it," I said, a little more forcefully this time.

I lowered my voice and it seemed to command her attention. As if someone had an invisible grasp on her neck, her head slowly panned over to meet my gaze. Her eyes were filled with fear. Anxiety. Worry. Which made me all the more determined to find out what that man had said to her.

"I've been charged with not only protecting you, but solving this case. Which means I need to work with all the facts at my disposal."

Watching closely, I saw her head nod as she took another sip of her coffee.

"I've seen the video footage. I know he came into the store behind you. And that he backed you behind that rack of jackets."

Watch her visibly shiver boiled my blood.

"I also know that you ran out in a panic and that he didn't follow you."

"He didn't? Good. Served him right," she said.

"I need to know what he said to you."

Diana closed her eyes before she shook her head.

"Diana, you have to tell me. I can't help you if you don't talk to me."

"You won't help even if I do talk with you. I'm enslaved and dragged around in imaginary chains because my father pisses someone off. No one can help," I said.

"I can help save your life and that of your father. But you have to talk to me in order for me to do that."

Her eyes fluttered open and I watched them redden before she cleared her throat. More real tears. Tears of fear. Real fear.

She seemed to be doing that more often.

"I have to know what I'm working with if I'm going to solve this case. The quicker I can get it solved, the quicker we can all be out of your life and you can go back home and resume things as normal," I said.

If I didn't know any better, I'd say that statement might have made her even sadder.

Chapter 6

Diana

How did my life get so out of control? When did everything start to crumble so quickly? Ethan kept asking me questions about the guy in the shop and I was shocked that he even knew about that. Then again, it shouldn't have shocked me. The second he told me he was able to pull camera footage, it all made sense. He was the police and the prison guard all mixed up into one. There probably wasn't anything he didn't know.

I wasn't sure if that thought comforted me or made me more worried.

Dropping my gaze to my coffee, I was unable to meet his eyes. I didn't want to see the look of concern on his face. It was all fake anyway. He didn't give a shit about me. All he cared about was wrapping up this job and leaving me with my father again. He'd just said it—the quicker he could get things solved, the quicker he could leave.

The quicker he could leave me behind.

"The man knew my name," I said.

"He called you by your name?" Ethan asked.

"He did. He asked me if I understood how dangerous this world was. He asked me why I'd given my father's private security team the slip."

"He said that. Those exact words?"

"No. I can't remember the exact words. But, yes. He knew the security detail was private, hired by my father, and that I'd ditched them. He knew my name, and he kept asking me if I was ready."

"Ready for what?"

"I don't know. He just backed me into that corner of jackets and kept getting closer and asking if I was ready."

My hands gripped my coffee mug tighter so they wouldn't shake in front of him. I looked up into Ethan's eyes and found his gaze boring into my face. I brought my coffee to my lips and took another sip.

"Do you know who that man is?" I asked.

I watched Ethan's face cloud over. Like an approaching storm with thunder off in the distance. He drew in a deep breath and parted those lips of his, but at that very second the damn waitress approached us.

"More coffee?" she asked.

"No, but you can take this salad away. I'm not hungry," I said.

"Diana, you have to eat."

"No, I don't. You can drag me anywhere you want, but I don't have to eat."

I pushed the plate towards the waitress and she cocked an eyebrow at me. She turned her back fully to Ethan and I watched his eyes widen before my face craned back to meet hers. She gave me this look. A wondering look. I knew the look. It was one that women gave to other women in public all the time. She was silently asking me if I was all right. If I needed help or assistance of any sort. I shook my head and she turned around, eyeing Ethan carefully before she picked up my salad plate.

"If you need anything at all, just flag me down," the waitress said.

Then she refilled our coffee mugs and retreated.

My stomach rumbled, but I ignored it. I wasn't eating anything this place had on the menu. Ethan's eyes followed the waitress all the way back to the kitchen, then he whipped back around and stared at me.

"Did she say anything to you?" he asked.

"Nope."

"What just happened? What was that?"

"An exchange between two women. She was making sure I was okay—with you."

"But you said she didn't say anything."

"She didn't have to. It's a look women give other women in public when they think they're in distress. You're a man, so I don't expect you to understand it. But women? We look out for one another," I said.

Like my mother looked out for me.

I watched Ethan nod before he settled back into the booth. He took a few bites of his food while we sat in silence and I had to admit, it smelled wonderful. I sipped on my coffee and tried to remind myself that his plate was laden with grease and fat, with absolutely no nutritional content. And if he ate like that all the time, it was a wonder he looked the way he did.

I bit down on the inside of my cheek and conjured his body up in my mind before his voice ripped me from my trance.

"We don't have an I.D. on the man in the store yet, but my team is working on it. And soon—just like everything else—we'll know everything about him."

Gazing into his eyes, I felt reassured by his words. A feeling of warmth filled my chest as I nestled into the bacteria-ridden booth cushion. That man in the store had spooked me more than I wanted to admit, and I believed Ethan. Despite all of the things we had been through and all of the shit I had pulled, I believed him from a professional standpoint. I knew he would keep me safe, even if it meant driving me nuts while he did it.

I watched him dig into his fried chicken and I turned my gaze back out the window. Mindlessly, I sipped my coffee, feeling its energy course through my veins. There was nothing around us. Nothing but trees, birds, fields and squirrels. We were in the middle of nowhere, and cut off from everything I had ever known. My hometown. My friends. My hangout spots. My shopping areas. There was nothing I recognized and nothing that excited me. Which only fueled my fears for what this safe house of his might bring.

"Well, when we get to the safe house, we'll be relying on our own cooking. And I don't know about you, but I flunked Home Ec. in school," Ethan said.

I had to fight back a smile as I shook my head. I knew what he was trying to do. He was trying to get me to eat. And so was my rumbling stomach. It didn't really matter that we would be relying on our own cooking. I'd spent more time with our personal chef at home than I had with my own father. I didn't cook much, but what I did cook was at least edible. If I needed to, I could get us through without starving.

Then, I heard a plate settle down in front of me.

"Found some fresher lettuce for you. And it turns out that our chicken is locally-sourced. From the farm two blocks up the road, actually."

I looked up at the waitress and found her studying me again.

"Are you sure you don't need anything else?" she asked.

"I can assure you, she's fine, ma'am," Ethan said.

"I sure as hell wasn't talkin' to you, sweet cheeks," she said, flatly.

I giggled as I looked down at the salad in front of me. I felt grateful for all the trouble she had gone to in order to put this together just because she thought I was in danger somehow. I picked up the balsamic dressing and poured it over the salad, then picked up my fork before my eyes turned back up to the waitress.

"Thank you. I really appreciate it. And yes, I promise I'm okay. I'm pissed off at my own circumstance, but otherwise fine and safe," I said.

I took a bite of the salad at the waitress nodded at me, then she shot Ethan one last look. The salad wasn't half bad. I eyed him playfully from across the table as he scoffed and shook his head, throwing his hands up as if he had given up on life. I rolled my eyes at him being so dramatic. And he called me a drama queen? The two of us fell into a silence that wasn't too bad and we finished up our meals. I was full, he was full, and the gas tank of the SUV was full. Ethan paid the bill and tipped the waitress well, then the two of us headed back to the car.

As we climbed back in, the tension between the two of us had been lessened just a tad.

The trees and the sound of the wind coupled with the gentle swaying of the car lulled me back to sleep. I had always been a sleeping passenger. Ever since I was little. Mom and I would take weekend trips to get away while my father was campaigning or holding luncheons to pander for money, and I always fell asleep on the way to our destination. It didn't matter where we were going, whether it was thirty minutes up the road or four hours across the state. I always fell asleep.

"We're here, Diana."

I felt something warm against my ear and I pressed myself against it. I heard Ethan's chuckle coat my eardrum and I moaned at the sound of it.

"Time to open those eyes. We need to get inside as quickly as possible."

His breath was hot and I felt my body rise to the occasion. Passion clouded my mind as my eyes fluttered open. I felt my nipples pucker against my bra as I blinked away the sleep from my eyes, ready to take in the shitty wooden cabin. It was probably swaying in the wind that rocked the SUV on its tires. No water. No electricity. No internet. Just a ratty, bed-bug ridden couch and a mattress we probably had to share.

That wouldn't be too bad, if Ethan wasn't such a dick sometimes.

But when I sat up in my seat and my eyes peeked out the window, my jaw hit the floor. I wasn't staring at some rickety wooden shack. I was staring at a proper country estate. A beautiful, sprawling estate, in fact. The house itself was white with crimson red shutters that matched the brick foundation of the house. It had a brick chimney crawling up the side and a brick walkway leading from the driveway we sat in all the way up to the front door. The antebellum estate had four columns on the facade of the house with rocking chairs and small tables littering the wrap-around porch. And as my eyes panned over the three-storied home, I realized something.

This damn safe house was bigger than my home in Georgetown.

It was a far cry from the shack I had been expecting and I scrambled out of the car to see more of it. I heard Ethan hoisting my luggage from the trunk as I stood there, dumbfounded. I didn't even try to hold in my shock. The smell of honeysuckle and persimmon trees filled my nose and I could have cried at the beauty of it all. At the sprawling green lawn and the beautiful and stately old trees that lined the property.

"Let's get you inside," Ethan said.

I watched him walk past me with all of our luggage in tow and I drew in a deep breath.

Maybe the man had a few surprises up his sleeve after all.

Chapter 7

Ethan

I watched shock roll over Diana's features as she took in my family's country estate. Shockwave after shockwave rolled over her adorable face and it made me grin. I buried my smile, knowing it wasn't appropriate for the moment. But she did look too cute with her jaw swinging and her eyes bulging. I knew she'd been expecting something much more rural. Possibly rundown, and off the grid, as well. Whatever it was she had concocted in her mind was bound to be terrible. I hoisted her bags into my arms and told her to follow me. I wanted to get her inside as quickly as possible.

Her gasp was audible, the second I threw open the front door.

Dropping our bags against the wall, I watched as she walked into the stately foyer. The white-washed walls and the dark mahogany hardwood floors welcomed her as a massive crystal chandelier hung from the ceiling. I closed the door behind her as her legs carried her mindlessly into the middle of the room. I watched her eyes sparkle with the crystal of the chandelier as it reflected in her gaze. I knew she didn't expect a man like myself to come from money. Especially more money than her father had. But I wasn't used to showing it off. Truck stop dinners were just as good—and maybe even better—than most five-star eateries.

Why?

Because they always felt like home to me.

My clients always wanted to take me out to all the expensive places, but I found that more times than not, the food was bland and tasteless. Price didn't always mean quality. Or quantity. At least, that was what my father had taught me. Sometimes a bit of butter and bacon fat made all the difference in the world to a dish, but a lot of those five-star restaurants wouldn't give you anything near that.

Not worth the money, in my opinion.

I considered my father's words as my eyes took in Diana. She walked around the foyer, taking in the artwork on the walls and the staircase that inched up the side of the room to the second floor. There would definitely be a high price to pay if I wanted to claim her as my own. But was she worth that price? Or would she burn me up and use me before dropping me once she got bored? That scenario was likely. Especially considering all the men pining away for her via unanswered text messages on her phone. But the thought of claiming her—the thought of burying myself in her body again—had been driving me insane since our hook up in the garden.

Now, I'd be locked away with her here until we could figure out who was threatening them, and I'd be closer to her than ever. Smelling her perfume everywhere I went, just like I had at her home. How the hell was I going to be able to resist her when there was absolutely nothing to do out here? How long until Diana's boredom would set in and she'd come after me for another measly distraction? I had to be strong and resist her. Resist the sway of her hips, the softness of her hair, the curl of her lips and the dip of her waist.

Thank fuck my house was bigger than hers.

As I picked up my things and headed for the large stairway, a voice stopped me in my tracks. A voice that permeated a warmth and a comfort over me. A voice that spread a smile across my cheeks.

A voice I'd loved since the day I had been born.

"Ethan? Is that you!?"

"Hey, Mom," I said, smiling.

"Oh my gosh! You're home!"

She came rushing down the hallway from the living room and I dropped my things. I wrapped her up into my arms and buried my face into the soft crook of her neck. Home. That was what my mother felt like. Smelled like. Home was wherever that woman was, and I held her tightly as she laughed into my ear.

"What in the world are you doing here?" I asked.

"Liam called me."

I groaned as a giggle left my mother's lips.

"I know, I know. You hate it when he does that. But he called me and said you guys would all be staying at the big house for a while and I just couldn't resist. There was nothing in the cupboards but the ghosts of mice past you know."

"So, you went grocery shopping," I said.

"Oh yes, I did. I bought groceries and stocked the pantry and whipped up some casseroles for you to pop in the oven. They're in the fridge when you need them, son."

I pulled back from my mother and cupped her cheeks.

"You do too much," I said.

"It's easier than teaching you how to cook," she said.

"Who is this?"

Diana's voice pierced the moment as my mother whipped around to take her in.

"Well don't be rude, Ethan. Introduce your mother to your lovely lady friend," she said.

"Your mother?" Diana asked.

I was going to kill Liam for calling my mother during something like this.

"Diana, this is my mother, Rebecca. Mom, this is Diana. My—"

"Client?" she asked.

"Yes," I said curtly.

"Oh, don't be mad at Liam. He knows he's going to be trapped here with you and your terrible cooking until you can get things settled out. It was an act of self-preservation."

"Your mother?" Diana asked.

I furrowed my brow at the tone of her voice. It was breathy. Shocked. But there was a sadness in it. Her eyes darted from me to my mother and back again before I watched emotions running behind her eyes. They ran so quickly I couldn't clock all of them. But I clocked some of them. Shock. Confusion. A deep-seated sadness.

My mother must've caught that, too, because she pulled away from me and slipped her arm around Diana's waist.

"Come on. Let's show you to your room," my mother said.

Diana looked back at me and I could've sworn I saw tears in her eyes again.

"You know, this house was built before the Civil War. It's been in our family the entire time. Renovated, remodeled and updated of course, but still the same beautifully bloodied bones from the South's torrid past."

I sighed as I picked up Diana's things and started up the stairs behind them. My mother knew every detail of history surrounding this house. And I loved my mother dearly. She was my rock. Especially after my father's death. But I didn't like her getting involved with my work. Yet another conversation I'd have to have with Liam. If we had been followed here, my mother could quickly become a target. If Liam hadn't told her I was coming, she wouldn't be here. She wouldn't be at risk. But the horse was out of the barn and I didn't expect her to start listening now, despite the danger. Rebecca Stark had never listened to anyone but herself before—including my sergeant father.

"The house has three stories and a basement. We're going to put you on the second floor in the finest guestroom. It's got a king-size bed with four posters and beautiful curtains that will reflect the sun and greet you with warmth instead of harsh rays. There's an ensuite bathroom stocked with goodies, like bubbles for your bath if you want to take one. The shower also has misters, so you can sit in there like a sauna if you want. And there's also a flat screen TV with movies and shows loaded for whenever you want to watch them.'

"Thank you. That's very kind," Diana said.

The softness of her voice caught me off guard and I whipped my head up. Then, I saw where my mother was leading her to.

Shit.

"Ethan can show you the basement, but there isn't much to it. It's basically a library with small electric fireplace and some places to sit. Nothing fancy, but if you like reading then that's the place to be," my mother said.

"What's on the third floor?" Diana asked.

"It's more like a large lofted space, really. Ethan can show you where the stairs are. There's a pool table up there and a small wet bar that is always stocked. There's a projection room with a popcorn maker and all sorts of flavors for it. I think there are a couple arcade games up there as well? I don't know though, I haven't been up there in a while. But there is also another smaller bedroom and a private terrace that opens up and overlooks the backyard."

"Sounds beautiful," Diana said.

"It is. It's my favorite spot in the house, when I can get by here. But let me show you into your room. Ethan can drop your bags in there and you can make yourself comfortable."

"Thank you. I really appreciate it," Diana said.

Her kindness kept flooring me. The sweetness of her voice entranced me. But the second my mother threw open that guest bedroom and I saw the way Diana fell in love with it, I knew I was fucked.

Because that room was right next to mine.

Chapter 8

Diana

I was in awe of Ethan's mother. Setting aside the fact that the two of them looked exactly alike, for the first time in my life I felt out-classed. Rebecca was classy. Definitely old money. She held herself with poise and grace and walked with her head held high. Even as we ventured up the steps, she moved more as if she was floating. And she had the cutest southern accent to go along with her lady's manners. She was beautiful from head to toe. Her long white hair was neatly formed into a bun at the crown of her head. I saw where Ethan got his icy blue eyes from, but on Rebecca they seemed warm and welcoming. Her smile was broad and her teeth were white. But not the artificial kind of white, like mine were from bleach. There was a genuineness to her I craved. A motherly feel to her touch that I had missed for so many years.

Her warmth reminded me of my mothers, and my heart both soared and broke at my feet.

The second she threw open the guest bedroom door, I was stunned. The massive four-poster bed boasted the softest mattress and sheets I'd ever seen. The room was huge. Bigger than even my mother's master suite. There was a sitting table near an old electric marble fireplace and a cushioned window seat that overlooked the backyard. The plush carpet gave way underneath my sandals as I scanned the walls, taking in the fifty-inch flat screen mounted on the wall.

But it was the bathroom that was a revelation.

It didn't have just any old tub. No, it was a huge, carved marble tub. It looked as if it had been made for two and my body ached to sink into it. The walk-in glass shower had chrome fixtures and misters galore recessed into the walls. The towels were plush, the double vanity was impeccable, and there was even a fluffy robe hanging behind the bath-room door just for me.

It was nicer than my room at home, and the money that dripped around me was intimidating.

I snickered as I looked at myself in the mirror. I looked like a wreck. No makeup. Mangled hair. Dirty clothes. Slightly sunburned skin. A twinge of remorse fell over me in that moment. I had been acting so entitled and stuck up all this time, when it was obvious that Ethan was far richer than my father every though about being. I'd been an idiot. I wondered what other surprises Ethan had hidden up his sleeve.

"If it isn't to your liking, we have other rooms you can—"

"This room is beautiful," I said breathlessly.

I tried to choke back my tears as best as I could as I turned to look into Rebecca's warm blue eyes.

How I wished she was my mother.

"Then I'll leave you to get settled in. Ethan, settle her things on the bed. She can unpack when she's ready."

I watched him hoist my things onto the bed before his mother pulled him out into the hallway. His eyes remained linked with mine until the last possible second, then the door was closed behind them both. I turned back to the mirror and looked at the pathetic excuse for a woman standing in front of me. I almost didn't recognize her, she looked so haggard.

"What an idiot," I murmured.

I wandered over to the door to pick up my purse and heard voices out in the hallway. I furrowed my brow and pressed my ear against the door, but I couldn't hear what they were saying. My hand reached for the doorknob and I silently inched it open. And when I peered out into the hallway, I watched the Stark family reunion unfold before my very eyes.

And ears.

"How have you been, son?" Rebecca asked.

"I've been fine. You know. Same as always," Ethan said.

"Is everything okay with the Logan's?"

"You know who they are?"

"Of course. I voted for her father during the last campaign year," she said.

"Well, you know I can't talk about it. It's business, and it's ongoing business."

"Are you sure there isn't anything I can do to help? I could stay behind. Maybe cook."

"No way. That isn't happening. You know what I do is dangerous, Mom. You're not stepping anywhere near it. I keep my business and my family life separate for a reason."

I heard Rebecca cluck at him before she picked an imaginary piece of lint off Ethan's shoulder. Every movement she made and every sound that fell from her lips reminded me of my mother. And it made my heart hurt.

"I just want to be a part of your life, sweetheart. You know this," Rebecca said.

"I'm not trying to shove you out of it. I'm merely trying to keep you safe," Ethan said.

"You're always tied up in business. You work too hard for your age. You really need to find some more time for your family life, you know. I miss you."

"I miss you too, Mom. But you know election years are always busy for my company."

It was clear Rebecca wanted to be a bigger part of Ethan's life, and it made me think about my own relationship with my father. There were days where he couldn't push me far enough away. When my father was far more interested in what he was doing than what I was doing. I wished my father was more like Rebecca. I wished my father took more interest in what I did with my life. Maybe if he did, I'd actually do something with it instead of aimlessly floating through life just trying to get his attention any way I could.

How pathetic had my life become?

"Well, anyway. Your client is very pretty," Rebecca said.

I saw her wink at Ethan and I had to bury my giggle. Even though a flush trickled up the back of my neck.

"She is," Ethan said.

Wait. Did I just hear him right?

Did he just admit to his mother that I was pretty!?

"Any chance for something more than a professional relationship?" Rebecca asked.

"Stop meddling, Mother," he said, as he shook his head.

Rebecca's laughter was soft. Elegant. Becoming of a woman of her stature. And yet, Ethan hadn't denied anything.

Oh my gosh. He didn't deny it.

"Well, if you aren't going to give up anything juicy to keep my ear attentive, then I guess I'll go home. But I'm coming back to check on you two in the morning," Rebecca said.

"No, Mom. I told you. You have to stay away from this until it's all said and done. I can talk about it afterwards. With Senator Logan's permission, of course," Ethan said.

"Pish-posh. I'll visit my own family whenever I damn well please."

Ethan laughed as Rebecca waved her hand in the air and the interaction filled me with a warmth my body hadn't experienced in years.

"Oh, and your little stunt? Putting Diana right next to my bedroom? Thanks for that," Ethan said sarcastically.

"Oh, you're welcome son. You know I always want to give our guests the best."

She picked at another imaginary piece of lint before tossing her son a wink.

"You're relentless, you know that?" Ethan asked.

"I'll see you in the morning," Rebecca said.

"I'm serious, Mother. Stay away from here until I can get this case wrapped up."

"What makes you think I'm coming just to see you?"

Her question made my ears perk up.

"What do you mean?" Ethan asked.

"Oh, son. You read people for a living. Can't you see that girl is in pain?"

Her words were like a punch to my gut. I watched Ethan's body turn and I quickly closed the door. Did he catch me? Did he see me eavesdropping? Lurking around listening in on their private conversation? I hoped not. I sat there with my back against the door and closed my eyes. I heard them murmuring. Talking. Interacting in a way my father and I hadn't managed without yelling since before my mother died. Then, I heard them laughing together as they both made their way down the stairs.

It felt like I had been found out. Like my greatest secret had been revealed. And Ethan had looked genuinely shocked at his mother's words.

I didn't know what to think. But I knew what I needed now.

I needed a damn shower.

Chapter 9

Ethan

I pulled my mother's chicken broccoli casserole out of the oven and heard footsteps descend down the hallway. Like always, the second I pulled the damn thing out of the oven, everyone would come tromping into the kitchen. Everyone loved my mother's cooking. Especially my team. They never got any home-cooked meals, since most of them were bachelors, which meant the best home-cooked meal they usually got was boiled noodles and canned spaghetti sauce. I set the casserole down on the table along with the homemade rolls and salad, then I watched as everyone began to pile food on their plates.

"Make sure to leave some for Diana. I'm going go to knock on her door," I said.

I poured us both a drink before I made my way up the stairs. I hadn't heard much from Diana since we had first gotten here yesterday. She had barely came down and hadn't made a peep. Other than bath water running and hearing her feet pad across the ceiling of the living room, there wasn't much to be heard from her.

Which was odd.

"Diana?" I asked.

I knocked on her bedroom door and heard her tell me to come in.

At least, I thought that was what she said. Her voice was so meek and soft that I couldn't really make out what she had said. I twisted the doorknob and slowly inched the door open. The sight before me felt like a blow to my chest. There was Diana, her wild raven hair flowing down her back and her legs curled up against her chest. She sat in the cushioned windowsill of her bedroom with her eyes fixed out on the backyard. Her expression was unreadable, but the longer she sat there, the harder she hugged her knees. Her back was hunched up and her eyes seemed glazed over, as if she was there, yet not really there.

Every time I thought I had her figured out, she surprised me with her vulnerability.

I stood there a moment to take her in. I hadn't realized her hair had any sort of kink to it. It was usually stick straight and smooth, but the wild jet-black hair in front of me was anything but tamed. It had beach waves in it reflecting the rays of the setting sun streaming through her window. She had on no makeup, her clothes didn't cling to her body, and her legs weren't shining with lotion. And yet, she was somehow more beautiful than the first time I had ever laid eyes on her.

How was that possible?

"Dinner's ready," I said as I cleared my throat.

"Not hungry," she mumbled.

"Well, my mother's cooking isn't something that's usually missed. If you don't come get any, I can't guarantee there will be any later for you to heat up."

I watched a small smile slide across her cheeks, but she didn't move. She didn't turn her head to face me and her eyes didn't connect with mine. She didn't get up from the windowsill and follow behind me. She didn't really make a move at all. And I didn't know what else to say to her.

But that didn't mean I wanted to leave her in the kind of mood she was in.

"Would you like to take a walk?" I asked.

The grin slid from her cheeks and her brow furrowed with confusion.

"It's just that we've been cooped up inside for a little while now. Either in the SUV or in the house. Figured you might want to stretch your legs," I said.

I wasn't sure if she would agree. If anything, reminiscing about what had taken place over the past twenty-four hours was sure to make her upset. But instead of kicking me out or throwing down another tantrum of hers, I watched her slide from the windowsill. She stretched her arms high into the sky until her back popped, then she bent down and touched her toes to stretch out her legs. I had to look away. Her languid movements were too much for me, even if she wasn't intentionally doing anything.

"Lead the way," she said.

I heard her fall in line behind me as I made my way down the steps. I ushered her out the front door while the guys all laughed and ate at the dinner table. I knew exactly where to take Diana walking. There was a path that ran across the massive backyard and into the woods that bordered the lawn. I placed my hand onto the small of her back until I had her feet falling on the cobblestones, then we followed the beaten path until we came to the edge of the woods. I felt her pull away from my hand and I allowed my arm to fall to my side, but the gesture wasn't tense or uncomfortable. In fact, nothing felt like that.

Not even the silence that hung between us.

I watched Diana's head pan around as she took in her surroundings. I watched the trees dance in her amber eyes. The awe and the amazement that hung in her features made me wonder how often she'd been outside of the city. Her feet slowly shuffled along the cobblestone before she stopped. I watched her bend down and pluck a wildflower from the side of the walkway before she brought it to her nose.

"That's a marigold wildflower," I said.

Her body came to a full stop as she closed her eyes and sniffed it.

"They're everywhere," she said, breathlessly.

"They grow wild and native around here in the summers," I said.

"It's beautiful. I've never seen anything like it."

A rush of excitement permeated through my veins. The idea of being able to show her new things made me feel proud. Especially things that had been important and vital to my childhood and my life as a whole. I started down the path again, eager to show her what I had carved out as a child. I hurried along the path and I felt her rushing to keep up with me as we entered the woods. I watched her frown in confusion, but I couldn't help it. This wooded path had always held a sort of magic for me. And I was about to show this magical place to Diana.

Something I thought she might enjoy.

"Why are we going so fast? Ethan, slow down."

"Almost there," I murmured."

"Almost where?" she asked.

The path finally dumped us into the clearing. The field I had spent so many hours of my childhood running around in. During the summer, it was bursting at the seams with wildflowers. I stopped at the edge and heard Diana shuffle up next to me as my eyes took it in. The yellows and the purples, the blues and the greens. The wildflowers swayed in the wind as it kicked up around us, and I heard her gasp as she took in the sight.

"Oh my gosh," she whispered.

I watched her take a step into the field as the flowers brushed against her calves. The evening sun beat down upon her olive skin, illuminating her in the colors of the sunset. She made her way slowly to the center of the field, and when we both got there I saw her eyes widen. In the center of the field was a small lake. And beside that lake was a small round stone building with columns and a dome roof on top. It was the gazebo my father and I had built when I was younger. It was a summer project of ours, and he had kept it up over the years.

Well, the years he was alive.

I walked up next to Diana and my eyes fell to her face. I watched her take it all in as the sunset was reflected in her brown gaze. Her parted lips broke into a heartbreakingly beautiful smile, and my breath caught in my chest. The wonder in her face and the newness of it all draping over her features—it was more than I could stand.

More than I could bear.

Diana was so fucking lovely, surrounded by the wilderness and the setting sun. I didn't regret for a second bringing her out here to see all this. I watched her take a step towards the stone building my father and I had built with our own two hands, and I followed directly behind her. Diana moved with grace and poise, but the tension was gone from her shoulders. She seemed more relaxed. More in tune with her surroundings. Not as uptight as she usually was.

She looked at home in this fanciful setting. And not even I could deny the beauty that idea afforded her.

Chapter 10

Diana

I had to admit, I was kind of digging walking through the forest. It wasn't something I'd ever done. Like, ever. And I didn't expect to like it. When Ethan suggested a walk, I figured he meant around the backyard or something. I didn't think he meant through the bushes and trees, or walking over sticks and dirt and leaves. It just wasn't my thing. Nature wasn't something that had ever appealed to me, I guess. I didn't go on hikes and I didn't go camping. I didn't enjoy swimming in nasty lakes. Hell, I didn't even enjoy swimming in public pools. The only water I enjoyed was the pool and hot tub at my father's house. And even then, the water had to be cleaned and disinfected and changed out frequently for me to get into it.

But when Ethan's beaten path with the sticks and the trees and the dead leaves finally broke, I was stunned with the sight in front of me.

It seemed to be an entirely different world. It sure as hell felt like it, anyway. The field was reminiscent of some kind of wondrous overgrown garden. Like the small little faction I tried to keep up at my father's house. Granted, I wasn't good at keeping it up. Things had grown up the side of the house and more plants died than lived, but I enjoyed the silence of it all.

Like the silence of the meadow in front of me.

Feeling the flowers brushing against my skin pulled me into another realm. I walked towards the edge of the lake, taking in the mirror as it reflected the setting sun for my viewing pleasure. The wind whipped around me, blowing my hair around and fluttering my loose shirt against my skin. I closed my eyes and took in the smell of the flowers.

Marigolds and sunflowers and roses and all sorts of others I didn't recognize.

They were more beautiful in the field than they ever could have been in any florist's shop.

It felt like something out of a fairy tale. The encased gazebo-like structure. The lake. The field full of flowers that rippled in the wind. It was as if I had jumped into a book, and I loved it. I held my arms out and felt the cool wind caress my hot skin, trying to stave off the sun as it pounded onto my skin.

"What is this place?" I asked.

I turned my head over towards Ethan as my arms dropped to my sides. And the smile he gave me reverberated through my bones and rattled my insides. I gazed into his icy blue eyes, only they didn't look icy any longer. They blended in with our surroundings. The blue of his gaze matched the sky above us and the blue flowers that peppered the field.

He was so damn handsome when he wasn't being a bossy asshole.

"This is a secret garden that was built by the same ancestor who built the house," he said.

"No, it's not. Really?" I asked.

"It is," he said with pride.

"So that gazebo over there is decades old."

"No. That gazebo is only—"

I watched him count out a little math in his head as a grin slid across my cheeks.

"Seventeen years old," he said.

"Who built it?" I asked.

"My father and I. We built it when I was a little boy. I thought it would be a nice addition to the lake and the flowers in the summertime. But it's just as beautiful in the winter."

"You and your father built that together?"

"We did."

"Wow. That's—"

I felt a pang of jealousy at that. I could never imagine my father spending that much time actually doing something with me.

"That's great, Ethan," I said.

"Our ancestors came from England, like most of the nobles in this area at the time. He purchased the land and built his home and it weathered more war and hatred than anyone could ever possibly imagine. And, like most nobles from England, he was obsessed with having the perfect garden."

"Must be a British thing," I murmured.

"Must be," he said, chuckling.

"The foundation for the gazebo looks older than the structure."

"Ah, you have a very good eye. That foundation was there when my father and I found this place when we were exploring one day in the woods. Turns out, there used to be a folly there, built with stones brought in from Scotland. Now, the folly didn't survive the war. But, the foundation did. So, my father and I used the original folly foundation and some of the original stones from Scotland to build the structure you see now."

I shook my head, unable to contain my shock at the story.

"Do you want to see it?" Ethan asked.

"I'd love to see it," I said.

He held out his hand for me and my eyes fell to it. He wanted me to take his hand? I was more shocked that I wanted to than the fact that he had offered. I slipped my hand into his and he smiled at me, causing my heart to skip a beat.

Then, he slowly led me over to the gazebo.

He escorted me inside and what I saw took my breath away, literally. There were several carved glassless windows to the outside of the structure, and there were stone benches set into the stone wall. I ran my hand along the wall, feeling the roughness of the stones and the concrete used to build this place. But it was the middle of the structure that took me aback the most.

There, in the middle of the encased gazebo, was a pit.

It wasn't really a pit. But I could tell the bottom was inlaid a bit. There was a patch of thick, plush carpet with pillows strewn about. It looked like a comfortable little hideaway. And it had the perfect view of the lake as the sun set below the trees. My eyes fell to the pillows, taking in their silken tassels and their plush comfort. I bent down to the edge of it so I could lean over and feel the carpet, but the second my eyes noticed something in the corner my attention was diverted.

There was something dark green among all the bright colors.

I reached over and picked up the foreign object, not knowing what it was as I grabbed it. When Ethan's chuckle hit my ears, it made me smile. I held an action figure between my fingers. A little soldier man standing at the ready for whatever action might come his way. I slid into the little hideaway and relaxed against the pillows, then passed the action figure over to Ethan when he did the same.

"This used to be one of my army men's headquarters when I was a child. I lost so many toys in that lake over the years."

I watched him study the little figure before he set it off to the side, his eyes growing unfocused. His memories were ripping him back. Taking him back to his childhood. I sat there with my legs curled underneath me, imagining what Ethan would have looked like as a boy. Playing with his action figures in a sea of silky pillows, battling it out against the evil forces of the world. Little Ethan, with his action figures and his wars, playing in his magical secret garden in a place he and his father built with their bare hands.

My heart melted a little more towards him.

"Were you and your father close?" I asked.

I watched his eyes grow weary before he let out a heavy sigh.

"We were," he said.

"You're lucky, you know."

His eyes panned over to mine as I relaxed a little more against the pillows.

"Not all of us are lucky enough to have memories like that with our fathers," I said.

"You don't have any with yours?" he asked.

"None I can really recall. Even before my mom died—"

I felt a knot catch in my throat and I focused my gaze on the sunset behind Ethan's head.

"You don't have to talk about it," he said.

"Thanks. Because I don't really want to," I said.

"But I do want you to know that people notice."

My eyes fluttered down to his as he pinned me with his gaze.

"People notice how your father treats you," he said.

I wasn't sure how to take that statement or how I needed to feel about it. So, I brushed it off. I nodded my head silently before my eyes fell down his body and I chastised myself for the movement. Heat pooled between my legs. My mind started to swirl with all sorts of things I could do to him in a place like this. But I tried to ignore the sudden rush of desire I felt for him. Especially with how things ended the last time.

Ethan needed to be off limits. No matter how perfect he seemed in the moment.

But the part of me that still longed for his touch couldn't stop wanting him. I closed my eyes and drew in a deep breath, forcing my gaze anywhere else. My eyes fluttered open and I found myself looking out the windows as I curled deeper into the soft pillows. And all the while, I was painfully aware of his gaze on my skin. His eyes raking over my body. His heat inching closer to mine. There was something about Ethan I couldn't shake. Something dangerous. And I wasn't merely talking about his sexy body.

I knew if we got involved and he broke things off, I would take the rejection hard. Probably harder than any rejection I'd ever experienced, though that wasn't much to begin with. He was alluring. Prideful, but in a good way. Commanding. Stern. But loving in all of his actions. I enjoyed all of that about him. It helped to settle my swirling mind and raging emotions when they kicked up and I couldn't control them.

But Ethan's breath against the shell of my ear pulled me from my trance.

"You're more beautiful than this garden or any flower in it, Diana."

I had no idea when he moved next to me, nor did I feel him slip his arm around my waist. But when I turned my eyes to meet his, our lips were mere centimeters apart. I felt his breath against my skin. I watched his eyes fill with a hungry light that made me shiver in his grasp. His fingers curled into my waist as I turned towards him, my body gravitating to him like a magnet to metal. My eyes fell to his lips. I watched him lick them lightly as I rose up onto my knees. Without thinking I maneuvered myself onto his lap and straddled his strong legs.

And my eyes never left his lips.

He let out a groan as I sank down onto him, his hands curling around my hips. My arms slowly threaded around his neck, bringing him closer as the sun beat down upon my back. Small fish jumped in the lake water behind us as the wind kicked up around the gazebo, and the symphony of nature blanketed our want for one another. My chest heaved as I felt his breath inching closer to my lips. Our foreheads connected as my fingers curled into the soft tendrils of his hair and I heard Ethan groan again.

Only this time, his groan was accompanied by an action that dragged me under his current.

His lips captured mine in a searing kiss as he dipped me back. His arms cloaked my body, holding me to him as his tongue slid against my lips. I welcomed his warmth. His taste. His radiance. I welcomed his fingertips encased in my excess and his arms pulsing against my back. I shivered as his tongue as it raked across the roof of my mouth. I didn't even attempt to hold myself back from the desire that crept through my bones.

I wrapped my body around his as he bent me back upright, my chest settling perfectly against his. Like two puzzle pieces locking together, my body molded to his every move.

And I never wanted it to stop.

Chapter 11

Ethan

I couldn't stop kissing her. I couldn't stop touching her. She called to me in those moments, when the sun soaked her skin and her eyes fell down my body. Just that one swoop of her gaze was enough to open up my world and I couldn't resist her any longer. I wanted her to know how beautiful she was to me. How wondrous she looked staring at the nature around her. But the moment her eyes dropped to my lips, I was done. It was too much, knowing how she wanted it. It was too much, feeling her crawl into my lap. And even though I had tried to keep my distance and tried to convince myself to ignore how I felt about her, I simply couldn't do it.

Seeing her in this gazebo—in my childhood playground—was too much for me. That sweet melancholy expression on her face. The way she sank into the pillows. The way she asked me questions and genuinely seemed to want to know the answers. The way she asked me if my father and I were close. The way she opened that vulnerable side of her just for a second. Just for me to experience alone.

It was a wonder I'd kept my hands off of her this long.

Now I couldn't help myself. As her lips swelled against my attack and her hips slowly rolled into my aching cock, I knew I'd never be able to stop. I couldn't bring myself to do it. My hands gripped her ass and I stood with her, climbing us both out of the cushioned pit. She moaned down my throat as my tongue caressed her cheeks. Her tongue. Her teeth. I sat her down onto one of the stone window sills and broke our kiss, trailing my lips down her cheek. I nibbled down her neck, feeling her shiver and sigh with delight as I made my way down to her chest.

I nuzzled my nose against the beading nipples beneath her thin shirt. I lapped my tongue over their clothed existence and the way Diana fisted my hair shot electricity through my cock. She pulled me closer to her chest. Closer to her pebbled tits as I wrapped my lips around them. I playfully bit down onto one and a moan fell from her lips. A moan that stiffened my cock as hard as a rock.

My hand slipped up her thighs, teasing the edge of her shorts. Her legs parted for me, silently begging me to continue my travels. I buried my face into her cleavage as I pressed underneath the trim of her shorts, praising the gods above that she had on loose clothes. I climbed higher and higher, desperate to touch her pussy. To fill her blazing heat with my fingers until she filled the fields of my childhood with the sound of my name. I felt myself drowning in her. I drank her in as her legs wrapped around my body. My lips shot back up to hers and she brought me in for a crashing kiss as my fingertips danced along her clothed pussy.

I lost myself in my desire for her, and come hell or high water I was going to feel her again

"Ethan," she whispered.

My back twitched at the sound of my name dripping from her lips. It was wrong, but nothing had ever felt more right to me. Her fluid body. Her long legs around my waist. Her hands fisting my hair and her lips pressed against mine. I wanted her. Needed her in a way I'd never experienced in my entire life.

"Diana," I groaned.

Then, my phone rang out from my pocket.

"Don't pick it up," Diana said.

I felt my hand falter between her legs as a frustrated sigh left my lips.

"I can't not answer it. It's probably one of the guys," I said.

"Please."

I moved my hand from between her legs, but she caught my wrist and stopped my movements. My eyes whipped up to hers and I saw her plea bleed across her features. It killed me inside because I didn't want the moment to end. I didn't want anything to stop us until we had both been satisfied. I wanted to paint this gazebo with our bodies. I wanted us to not stop until the flowers of the field knew nothing but our names.

But she was my client, and I was her security. Which meant I had people to answer to.

People I couldn't ignore.

Sadness filled her gaze as I moved my wrist away from her grasp. I pulled myself away from her as I shoved my hand into my pocket so I could answer my phone. I didn't even bother to see who was calling. I was too focused on the way Diana turned and curled herself back up onto the windowsill. Closing herself off again. Focusing her gaze off into the distance. Curling her legs up to her chest and hugging them tightly.

The same stance she had in her room when I first found her.

"This is Ethan," I said.

"Ethan. It's Senator Logan."

"Hello, Senator. How can I help you?"

"I wanted to uh, check on my daughter. How's she doing?"

"She's doing fine. It's an adjustment, being out here. But we're all making it."

"So uh, she's good?" he asked.

I furrowed my brow at his question.

"Yes, Senator. She's good. Nothing has changed since we talked last night."

"Good. That's good," he said.

"You sound distracted. Is everything okay?" I asked.

"I wanted to call and let you know that I might be a little delayed after the recess."

"What do you mean, sir. It's imperative that—?"

"An unexpected business meeting has come up? I have attend bef9re I can come down to, you know, where you are."

"With all due respect, Senator, this was not the deal."

I heard Diana scoff as she shook her head to herself. And for once, I could sympathize with her reaction.

"Well, I've already agreed to the meeting. It's only a day's delay," the senator said.

"Sir, you're my client. And you're in danger. What you need to be doing is focusing on saving your life rather than attending a business meeting," I said.

"Good luck," Diana murmured.

My eyes turned to her body and I watched her slump her back against the stone wall.

"Now you listen here, Stark. My business interests don't wait. They can't. This is my career, and just as I don't meddle in yours, you don't meddle in mine."

"And you listen to me when I tell you that you've been doing nothing but meddling in my job since you first hired me. You're not going to that business meeting. You're coming to this safe house. Once Congress goes into recess, you'll get in that SUV and you'll get down to this safe house. Are we clear?"

"You sound just like your old man, barking orders when you think no one hears you."

"Charming," I said flatly.

I heard the senator sigh over the phone as Diana's head nodded mindlessly. Holy hell, if this was what she had put up with her entire life, no wonder they had such a shit relationship.

"Is there anything else, Senator Logan?" I asked.

"No. There isn't," he said, curtly.

"Then I'll see you at this safe house once Congress is in recess."

I hung up the phone, unmoved by the Senator's sarcastic charm. I stuffed my phone back into my pocket, the mood between Diana and myself officially ruined. I sighed and gazed over at her as the last of the sun began to set and I knew we needed to be getting back. The trail got very dark at night, and even the flashlight I had on my hip wouldn't completely light our way back.

"Come on. Let's get home," I said.

I went to go help Diana from the windowsill, but she slid down herself. She exited the gazebo without a second thought or a word tossed my way and my head fell back. Fuck. The moment had been perfect. The situation had been perfect. The tension between us had been damn near perfect.

I'd be kicking myself about this one for days to come.

We both walked in silence as I led her back to the house. And even as her eyes fluttered along the forest floor, I could tell she was lost in her own thoughts. She wasn't alone in that venture, either. I was already in my own head. I couldn't believe I had done it again. Given into my desires when it came to Diana. And this time, it hadn't even been her fault. In the back of my mind, I knew exactly why I led her out to that garden. Sure, it was to show her a part of me. Sure, it was to stretch her legs. But deep down? Honestly, I had wanted that moment to happen between us. I had wanted to see if that spark was still there.

So, I was definitely a piece of shit. And I'd have to work even harder not to surrender to my lust for her again. Because it was apparently going so far as to concoct scenarios to make it easier for us to fall into one another's arms.

I led her through the front doors and she took off for the stairs. I stood there until I heard her bedroom door shut, and that was that. She didn't come down to heat up leftovers and she didn't come out to talk. She stayed in her room all night and I didn't hear a sound out of her.

Not until the next morning.

The smell of coffee wafted underneath my nostrils as I shuffled into the kitchen. And when I saw Diana standing there, pulling a mug from the cabinet above the coffee maker, I stopped in my tracks. There she was, with sleep-tousled hair, cotton pajama bottoms that barely covered her ass, and a shirt that kept lifting up and exposing her skin every damn time she moved.

My mouth felt drier than it ever had in my life.

I was shocked to see her in the kitchen just after sunrise, especially since she wasn't an early riser. I watched her reach up for another empty mug and I looked around, trying to figure out who she was getting coffee for.

"Figured you might want some," she said.

She slid the mug out to her side and I walked over to get it. The air between us was thick. Tense. Awkward even, just for a moment. I watched as Diana poured herself a cup of coffee before handing the pot to me, then I watched her reach for a bowl of grapes she had apparently helped herself to.

"Nice to see you eating," I said.

She popped a grape into her mouth before she sat back against the kitchen counter.

"What are the plans for today?" she asked.

"Well, I've got a meeting with my team this morning after we all eat breakfast, then I plan to spend the day working."

"On what?"

My eyes whipped up to hers and I found her staring at me. Not with amusement, but with curiosity. Genuine curiosity. The situation felt oddly domesticated.

And it worried me that it felt comfortable.

"We're still working on trying to determine the identity of the man who confronted you in the clothing store. That's my current priority," I said.

I watched Diana's face slide into something akin to disappoint-ment, but I didn't know why. She didn't say anything about it, so I let it fall to the wayside. I was long past trying to figure out why she felt the way she did most times.

More important to me were the actions and scenarios that triggered those emotions in the first place.

"Well, enjoy your breakfast," Diana said.

I watched her pick up her bowl of grapes and grip her mug as she padded out of the kitchen. I wanted to call out and stop her. To tell her to come back and tell me why she was so disappointed in my answer. But a familiar voice that filled me with frustration emanated from be-hind me.

"Good morning, Ethan."

"Hello, Mom."

I felt her slide her arms around my waist and press her cheek to my back.

"What are you doing here, Mom?" I asked.

"Just figured I'd slip in and cook you guys some breakfast," she said.

"Didn't I tell you to stay away?"

"It's just breakfast, son."

"I'm working, Mom."

"I hear you, son."

I shook my head and bit down onto my lip as she released me from her grasp. She made her way to the fridge and opened it up, then began pulling things out. Bacon. Eggs. Milk. Cheese. Butter. She set about the kitchen, throwing bacon in a pan and scrambling up nearly two dozen eggs for my men to devour.

She tossed bread into the toaster and pressed it down before she cleared her throat.

"So, how'd you sleep?" she asked.

"Fine, Mom."

"Get any good work done?"

"You know I can't talk about that, Mom."

"You can drop the tone. I know my name just fine by now," she said.

"Am I going to have to change the locks on the house to keep you out?"

"Not when there's a cellar I can access."

I chuckled and shook my head as the smell of sizzling bacon filled the kitchen.

"That bacon?" Liam asked.

"Of course, he'd wake up to the smell of bacon," I said.

"What? I like bacon," he said.

"Good morning, Liam," my mother said.

"Morning, Mrs. Stark."

"Get over here and give me a hug," she said.

I watched Liam walk over to my mother and wrap her up tight.

"How did you sleep?" my mother asked.

"I slept fabulously. You know I always do on these beds," Liam said.

"See? That's a good answer for your mother," she said.

"Ah, don't worry about Ethan. He's wound up tight with this case. He needs to relax a bit."

"That's what I keep telling him. Come home and let me cook and clean for him for a little bit. Put his feet up. Have a drink. Zone out to some television."

"Can I come home and let you cook and clean for me?" Liam asked.

"Only if you promise not to do any work while you're there," she said, smiling.

Liam wrapped my mother up into another hug before he plucked a piece of bacon from the drying rack. He plopped it into his mouth before he turned and winked at me, which sent my eyes rolling. That man would sell his soul for a plate of bacon, and I knew he was buttering up my mother for more.

But what I really needed from her was to stay as far away from this house as possible until I could get things figured out with this case.

Chapter 12

Diana

I spent the entire weekend bored to tears. At first, I tried filling my time by wandering the halls of the mansion I was trapped in. And I actually discovered some interesting areas. I ventured down into the basement where the library was and I found that Ethan's mother had really downplayed its grandeur. The basement spanned the entire length of the house and had just as many corridors as the main floor. And every single space was filled with books. Bookshelves were built into the walls and some were tacked on after the fact. There were chairs and beds and couches built up on more bookshelves that were stuffed full with paperback pages. I ran my hands along their dusty spines and felt a tug in my gut. They looked neglected. Forgotten about.

I knew how they felt.

After I found my way up to the third floor of the house, I ran my fingertips along the green felt of the pool table. I made my way through the small bedroom and out onto the private terrace that overlooked the entire property. Nothing but beautiful green lawns and trees spanned for miles. There wasn't even another house around, as far as I could tell. It was a beautiful sight, and I stood there admiring it for a while.

Then, I ventured into the movie room.

I made myself a small batch of caramel popcorn and flopped down into one of the leather recliners. I had myself a little movie marathon, watching the first two Pitch Perfect movies. I sang along to the songs and tossed popcorn between my lips. But when the movies wound down and the popcorn was gone, I was back to exploring.

Making my way outside, I explored the grounds. Not without someone following me, of course. It seemed that wherever I looked outside, there was a man watching me. A man in black with a gun on his hip and sunglasses on his face. They couldn't have been anymore obvious or stereotypical. At least change up the color of the suit or something. I shook my head and kept walking around, taking in the flowers that brushed against my ankles.

Part of me wanted to go back to the secret garden. But I really didn't want to go back without Ethan.

Other than those areas, there wasn't much else to do. I made my way back to the screening room and watched a bit of reality television. That grew boring quickly, though. Reality T.V. was more up Harper's alley. Especially with her wanting to be famous one day. She'd been trying to get herself on the newest reality television series for rich kids in D.C. I couldn't remember what it was called, but Harper spent considerable time pondering her 'big break moment.'

I watched reality television with her to appease her, but I didn't really care for it myself. Too much drama.

And I had enough of that in my world.

Feeling antsy, I was tired of being cooped up in the house. Ethan had been working non-stop, and every time I turned a corner he found a reason to move into another room. As if he was avoiding me. That didn't shock me, though. That seemed to be his M.O. Take me in private, reject me in public. Like his dirty little taboo secret. That didn't stop it from hurting, though. It didn't stop the action from driving me insane. Every time I found another place to settle down and explore, my mind drifted back to our make-out session in the gazebo.

Our gazebo.

I knew better than that. It wasn't 'our' anything. It wasn't our gazebo or our garden or our lake. It was all his and his families and I had only been privy to it because of a moment of weakness on his part. It didn't stop the moment from being any less fiery and beautiful, though.

Reminiscing on it was a mistake. It had driven me crazy. Crazy for him. Crazy for his body. For his touch. For his lips.

For those arms that knew exactly how to hold me close, though they knew all too well how to let me go.

By the time Sunday afternoon rolled around, I threw caution to the wind. I grabbed a corkscrew from the kitchen before I wandered down into the small wine cellar and grabbed a bottle of very fine red wine. I pulled a glass from a hutch by the bottles and made my way back up to my room, determined to enjoy what I could of this place. I scurried into my bathroom and drew myself a hot bath, tossing some of the lavender bubbles into the running water. The scent filled the room as I popped open the bottle, then I poured myself a generous glass. If no one was going to keep me company, then my wine would. After soaking in a nice, hot bath, I knew I would feel a lot better about myself and my current predicament.

After all, the carved marble tub had been calling to me ever since I'd first laid eyes on it.

I peeled my clothes away from my body and tossed them into the room. Then I grabbed my wine glass, set the bottle next to the tub, and submerged into the soft bubbles. I groaned with delight, feeling every single one of my muscles relax under the heat of the water. I reached up with my toe and shut the water off, then listened to the bubbles popping as I sipped my wine.

And dear sweet heaven, it was good wine.

I quickly tore through the first glass then refilled it to the top, committing the label of the wine to memory. It was one I definitely wanted to find when I finally got back home. The alcohol loosened up my body and I sank myself deeper into the bubbles, allowing my eyes to fall closed.

And the minute they did, Ethan's face appeared in my mind's eye.

Why in the hell would God send me such a sexy security guard and then expect me to keep my hands to myself? Why would God send me such a beautiful, strong specimen—who was everything I'd ever looked for in a man—and then make him wholly and completely uninterested in me? Was it some cruel joke? Had I fucked up in a past life enough to warrant this torture? I took deep pulls from my wine glass as the bubbles popped against my skin, and the more I drank the more my mind began to wander.

I thought about what might have happened if my father hadn't called Ethan when he had. I started wondering where Ethan's fingers would have gone next had his damn phone not rang out. Would he have kept going? Would he have stopped himself anyway? Would he have slowly pulled my clothing off before tracing my body with his tongue? Would he have tasted me greedily, devouring my juices until I called out to him?

Maybe I should have gone to my knees on that plush carpet and tasted him.

I felt my nipples puckering at my thoughts and took another sip of my wine. I spread my legs, imagining his commanding hands parting my thighs. I still felt his lips on my neck. Nibbling my skin and making his way down to my breasts. The way his tongue felt over my clothed nipple was enough to move my hand. I slid it over my stomach and down my pelvis, my fingers venturing towards my swollen clit.

It had been aching for attention ever since Ethan's warmth beat down onto it in the garden.

I set my glass of wine off to the side and cupped my breast. My fingers parted my folds as my leg was tossed over the edge of the tub. I imagined feeling Ethan's cock pulsing against my thigh as I straddled him against the pillows. I still tasted him on the tip of my tongue as my fingers slowly circled my clit.

Then, my mind flew back to our moment in the garden. Where his hand ripped open my sweatpants and he filled me without a second thought.

"Oh, Ethan," I groaned.

The power he held over my body. The way his hand gripped my hair and the way he made me keep his eyes on him. There was something intimate about it. Like he wanted my eyes to keep reminding him of what was happening. I felt him filling me. Electricity buzzed throughout my body. My fingers moved faster, jiggling my legs as bubbles popped against my skin. I panted as I conjured his kiss. His soft lips against mine. His hands moving everywhere. Pinching my nipples, massaging my breasts, and splaying across my back. I felt him filling me. I saw him doing it in my mind. Bucking against me before he picked me up, ripped at my overgrown roses, and pressed me against the side of my own damn house.

Desperate for me, like I had been for him.

"Ethan. Oh, yes!"

I saw his cock sliding in and out of me. I felt my pussy swallowing him down. I squeezed my eyes shut and arched my back, desperate to place my tits against his face. I loved it when he buried into my bosom. Loved it when he sank his teeth into the meat of my breasts. I moved my fingers faster and faster, then dropped down and filled my pussy with them.

"Take me, Ethan. Have your way with me, please."

I bucked against my hand, imagining Ethan's massive dick diving in and out of my juices. His thick cock filling me, desperate to pump me full of his cum. My body bucked. My legs contracted. My toes curled and my calves began to cramp. My jaw unhinged as my movements faltered, growing choppy as I gasped for air. I wanted Ethan to fill me. I wanted him to take me in every position possible. I wanted him to bend me over my bed and fuck me against the wall and slowly rock with me in his lap until we both came together, covered in each other's sweat.

"Yes. Yes. Yes. Right there. Right there. Right there."

I lifted my hips to my fingers and felt myself unravel. I came undone in the bathtub, filling the water with my juices. They fled from my body as I pushed my own hand out. My fingers traveled back up to my clit and circled slowly, riding out my orgasm as my head fell to the back of the tub. His name fell from my lips. I chanted it like a desperate prayer, hoping he would magically appear in the room and take me in his arms. Kiss me like he always did.

Make me his like he had in the garden beside my house.

I collapsed into the water, sweating from my exertion and spent from my pleasure. The command that man had over my body didn't even require his presence. A sloppy smile spread across my cheeks as I grabbed my wine glass, filling my mouth with its alcoholic euphoria. And all the while, one phrase echoed off the corners of my mind.

You're more beautiful than this garden or any flower in it, Diana.

But I was quickly ripped from my trance when a groan hit my ears. A groan that oddly matched the voice echoing off the chambers of my mind.

Chapter 13

Ethan

Dinner was ready and Diana was nowhere to be found. Everyone came to sit at the table for another one of my mother's infamous casseroles as I headed for the stairs. I knew where Diana was. I'd heard the water running earlier and hadn't heard anything since. One of the wine glasses was also missing from the cabinet, which meant she must have really been enjoying herself in the bathtub.

I walked up the stairs and knocked on her bedroom door, hoping she would hear me from the bathroom. But when I got no response, I stood there and listened. I didn't hear a thing. No sloshing of the water. No padding of bare feet. No murmuring of Diana's voice. I didn't want to barge in on her privacy if she was in the bathtub, but every single worst-case scenario started running through my mind.

I backtracked down the hallway and took the steps up to the third floor. I looked around the pool room and the entertainment room. I even made my way out onto the balcony and looked over the edges of the property. I ran back downstairs and brushed past the men at the table, and I felt them all looking at me as I ripped the basement door open.

"Stark, you good?" Liam asked.

"If Diana isn't in this basement, I need men scouring the property," I said.

"Wait a second, what?" he asked.

"I need you guys to put your stomachs on hold for a second and check the grounds of the property. I can't find Diana anywhere and I'm not sure what's happened."

My men all scrambled from the table and Liam quickly divided them into teams. I dropped myself into the basement and turned on every light so I could thoroughly check the downstairs. I made my way into the wine cellar and my eyes cased the wall. Looking for any clues as to what Diana might be doing. I came across an empty hole in the wall where a bottle of wine would have been.

Missing bottle of wine. Missing glass. Bathtub that had water running in it a little while ago.

Everything told me she was in that damn tub, but it was unlike her to be so quiet. But when all of my men came back and told me they couldn't find her on the property, Liam asked the one question that worried me more than anything.

"You think she left the estate?"

"If she did, all of you are losing your jobs," I said.

"I'm going to go ahead and assemble a team to go out searching for her," Liam said.

"I've got one more place I want to look. And if she's not there, that's exactly what we're doing," I said.

My heart slammed in my chest as I made my way back up the steps. I felt all of my men gathered at the bottom, waiting on my command. My heart dropped to my toes as I inched her bedroom door open. Maybe there was a note in her room somewhere. Telling me where she was or that she wasn't coming to dinner. After all, she knew where that garden was. Maybe she had made her way back out there with the wine.

That was a total possibility.

I looked all over her room before my eyes fell to the closed bathroom door. Well, it wasn't latched, but it was practically closed. There wasn't a light shining underneath the door and I didn't hear Diana moving around, but something tugged me towards it. I felt my feet carrying me slowly, my eyes locked onto the barrier between myself and the tub I knew I heard running beforehand.

Then, I heard it.

Water splashing over the edge.

I reached my hand out and slowly inched the door open, but for some reason I didn't say a word. My eyes fell to the reflection in the bathroom mirror and I instantly swallowed my tongue. There Diana was, with the wine bottle on the floor and the wine glass on the edge of the tub. She was sitting in a bath full of bubbles with the lights off and her leg tossed over the edge. Her olive skin was flushed. One of her hands gripped her breast. Her other hand was underneath the water, slowly moving around, and I knew exactly what she was doing.

And I couldn't peel my eyes away from her.

"Take me, Ethan. Have your way with me, please."

The moan she let out forced my cock to heights I'd never experienced before. My pants became uncomfortable as my name fell from her lips. I watched her buck against the water. I heard her praise the 'massive dick' I apparently had. Her toes curled and her legs began to shake and she lifted herself out of the bubbles completely. I saw her fingers filling her juicy pussy. I felt my cock leaking against my fucking pants. Her jaw unhinged and she gasped for air, chanting her pleasure she rode herself to her high.

"Yes. Yes. Yes. Right there. Right there. Right there."

I watched her collapse into the water, dripping with sweat and panting for air. Her hand fell from her perfect breast as her chest flushed with a want for more. Her tits puckered to painful peaks I wanted to wrap my lips around and her leg slowly slid itself back into the tub. I watched a lopsided smile cross her cheeks as she reached for her wine glass, and the second she wrapped her lips around it a groan slipped from mine.

An involuntary groan that caught her attention.

"What the hell are you doing!?"

My eyes found hers in the reflection of the mirror as she quickly sank all the way into the tub. Nothing but her head was seen poking up from the bubbles and her hands still trembled from the force of her orgasm.

Holy hell, my cock physically hurt, pressing against my pants. And it forced me to grit my teeth.

"I'm sorry. We were looking for you and couldn't find you," I said hurriedly.

"So you thought you'd spy on me?" Diana asked.

"Dinner's ready."

She scoffed and shook her head as she took a long pull from her wine glass. "How long were you standing there?"

I cleared my throat. "Just now." I couldn't stand there a second longer. If I did, I'd join her in that tub and show her what my cock could really do. I knew I sounded lame. Like some bumbling idiot. And it would only make things worse if I continued to stand there. I quickly shut the bathroom door and retreated down the hallway, then leaned against the wall to catch my breath.

Holy shit. That was the hottest thing I'd seen since—well, since the last time I had touched her.

"You find her?"

Liam's voice ripped me from my trance and I looked down the stairs at my men.

"You look like you just went nine rounds with her," Liam said, grinning.

"Yes, I found her. No, she's not happy. Yes, you guys can go eat," I said.

"Fair enough," he said.

They all dispersed and I was thankful for it. That meant I could shove my hand into my pants and rearrange my cock. Fuck. I hoped none of my men saw that thing. It was hard enough to pound nails, and I ducked into a room so I could get control of my appearance.

So I could situate myself in silence.

I stood in my bedroom and drew a few deep breaths. Walking into my bathroom, I splashed cold water in my face. I even tried to think about work. Anything to distract myself from the memory of Diana masturbating and calling out my name. And it took forever. Even though I rearranged myself and even though it didn't technically look like I had a raging erection, I sure as hell wasn't going downstairs and eating with my men while I had one. By the time I got myself under control enough to look presentable, however, Diana was the only one left at the dinner table.

Damn it. How long had I been in my room?

She flashed me an angry glance before she got up from the kitchen table. She brushed past me, rolling her eyes and shaking her head. She stood at the kitchen sink and rinsed her plate off, then bent over and stuck it in the dishwasher.

I already felt my cock rising back towards the occasion.

"I'm really sorry, Diana. I didn't mean to intrude on your privacy."

Watching her reflection in the kitchen window, her frown overtook her face.

"I had a feeling you might have been in the tub, so I had the guys search the grounds completely before I resorted to opening your bedroom door," I said.

"Is that supposed to make me feel better?" she asked.

"No. I just don't want you thinking I did it on purpose."

"Oh, so you weren't spying on me in the tub on purpose."

She rolled her eyes as she closed the dishwasher, then turned around and leaned against the counter.

"I really didn't mean to intrude on your privacy," I said.

"I don't have privacy here, Ethan. Which is surprising, since I've been alone for days while you guys are all barricaded in your precious office space."

I watched her push away from the counter and she left the kitchen without a second thought. For some reason, her words had really bothered me. Yes, she had been cooped up here with no attention. There wasn't anything I could do about that. We had work to do and she needed to be kept safe. Out of the public eye. But if there was one thing Diana hated, it was being ignored. The interesting thing was, I felt the need to do something for her.

And that was different.

She had put up with a lot. She'd been ripped around and commanded to do all sorts of things that would make any person crack under pressure. And my desire to do something for her to take the edge off grew stronger the more her footsteps backtracked from me. She had been putting up with a lot. Being alone throughout the day. Not having a car to go do things. Being in the woods in a place she was wholly unfamiliar with. She deserved a treat. Especially since her captivity hadn't caused her to lash out. She hadn't attempted to run away or combat any of the men, and she sure as hell hadn't thrown any sort of tantrum.

A treat would be good for her.

And I was excited to give her one.

Chapter 14

Diana

S itting in the SUV with a smile on my face, my leg jiggled with delight. I still couldn't believe it. I was going into town for the first
time in four days. Ethan had surprised me at breakfast with the sugges-
tion that we go into Abington and have a look around. I was so relieved
to get out of that damn house. Ever since we'd arrived a few days ago, I
had been surrounded by Ethan's family environment. Surrounded by
confusing feelings I had to accept and process. Surrounded by a lifestyle
I secretly wished I lived. I had always been a city girl and I knew I would
never get that chance. But I was surprisingly comfortable on the Stark
family estate.

I had even started envisioning what kind of life I could have lived
there. Which meant I was slowly losing my mind.

Thank fuck we were going into town. It was just what I needed to
clear my mind of all the insanity that had taken place in my imagina-
tion.

"This is the main strip of Abington. This is where everyone from
the outlying towns comes when they're looking for a good time," Ethan
said.

I wiggled around in my seat with excitement as my eyes were glued
out the window. But the second he turned onto the 'main drag,' my excitement began to wane. Main Street was nothing but a ghost town. It
had nothing on it. It was less than a dozen blocks long and dotted with
maybe that many stores. And those stores were ancient at that. Most of
them being thrift stores. Was Ethan kidding? He had to be pulling my
leg. There was no way this place was the main drag of anything.

But the more we rolled down the road, the more serious he became. There were dimly-lit restaurants and signs with cobwebs on them. Half of the damn shops were closed and boarded up anyway. It was a far cry from the main drag of D.C., and by the way his eyes lit up as we drove through, one would have thought we were in downtown New York City. I felt Ethan ease the SUV into a parking space before he came over and opened my door, and part of me didn't want to get out.

Part of me wished I would have just stayed in the damn house.

"Come on. It isn't as dreary as it looks. I promise," he said.

I scoffed and shook my head as I slid out of my seat.

"Whatever you say," I said.

"Like this shop, for instance. It looks like a plan old thrift store. Right? Dusty. Full of old, musty shit."

I giggled and shook my head as he escorted me onto the sidewalk.

"Well, this stretch of buildings has been here since the Civil War."

"Seems like everything is that way in the South," I said.

"This particular store served as a medical house for the wounded. It catered to both sides, actually. The Union and the Confederacy. There's a small place in the back of the store where if you go and stand underneath the light, you can see some of the bullet holes that still taint the wood from the gunshots of opposites sides trying to take out the doctors that wanted to help, no matter the side."

"Really?"

"Really," he said.

"Can we go see it?"

He smiled down at me and I felt something lurch in my chest. We walked into the thrift store and headed straight back, and I couldn't believe my eyes. There was a light on in a back room with a small video playing on loop, and there were holes plastered in two of the four walls that surrounded us. A commemorative plaque hung on one of the untainted walls, but I couldn't rip my eyes away from the holes.

The small, round holes that boasted of more history than the entire building itself.

Ethan escorted me down the street, rattling off facts and pointing out the historical features of the town. We walked into the soda shop to get a root beer float and he told me all about how that shop had a cellar underneath that helped with the Underground Railroad. We walked across the street to the museum that was open and Ethan educated me on how that small building was the site of Virginia's first ever interracial marriage. We ducked into the library and found ourselves in the historical section, pulling out books and reading up on the history of the town.

We even stood outside a tiny cafe, where the woman sweeping dust out onto the street smiled and greeted us with warmth. Then, she offered for us to come inside and have a slice of pie.

"We just had some floats from Dan's shop down the way, but we'll be back for lunch, Miss Ethel. I promise," Ethan said.

"The two of you better be back. I've got my chocolate mousse pie and my blackberry cobbler cooking right now," Miss Ethel said.

"Oh, then we will definitely be back," Ethan said.

I was in awe of their warmth. Of their welcoming smiles and their kind eyes. I'd never gotten this type of friendly invite in D.C. without spending money in a shop somewhere. But people here, they were kind whether you had money to spend or not. Hell, they were kind to me even though they didn't agree with my father's politics.

It was like I'd stepped into another dimension or something.

Ethan turned us down a side street where there were a slew of small black and white signs hanging in front of the offices lining the street. The shopping in Abington was a far cry from what I was used to, but for some reason I didn't feel the need to shop or spend money. For some reason, I was content just walking the sidewalks with Ethan, talking to all of the shop owners, and allowing my eyes to do a bit of window shopping.

It was strange and unfamiliar, and I liked it a lot.

We turned down side street after side street, encountering a ton of small shops. There were a few boutiques with quirky names and colorful signs that made me smile. I felt Ethan's hand press into the small of my back, guiding me up to the doorstep of a boutique called 'Southern Gentleladies.' When we got into the store, I felt a little lost.

None of the clothes that lined the walls were the cutting-edge designer styles I was used to. But the fabrics were still beautiful. Silken. The dresses were flowy and had intricate designs on them. I walked over to a dress that caught my eye. A spaghetti-strapped dress that swirled with bold colors. It felt soft in my hand. Breathable, which was probably perfect for the southern humidity.

"Here, try this on," Ethan said.

I felt something plop down onto my head before it ate my vision. I pushed the massive hat up my head and turned to look in the mirror before I shot Ethan an incredulous look. He couldn't be serious. The damn thing was way too big for me. It's massively wide brim practically fell into my face and the wiry pink bow was practically the size of my head. But the second a grin breached his cheeks, I knew he was joking.

And the two of us shared a nice laugh.

Walking around the store with him, I put up with how he tossed clothes onto my form. Sometimes another hat came down onto my head and sometimes a scarf worked its way around my neck. And every time, we'd laugh. I put a hat on him and we pranced around the store, slipping into playful southern drawls while we tried on gaudy jewelry and fawned over the fake jewels in the rings that were way too big for my fingers anyway.

"Oh, this would match that rainbow thing on your finger perfectly," Ethan said.

A scarf came down around my neck again, but it wasn't the same scratchy material like the others. It was oddly soft. And the design was beautiful. I slid all of the jewelry off and slipped the hat from my head, then went and studied myself in the mirror. I tied the silken scarf off into a little bow around my neck, finding myself taken by it.

But when I looked at the price, I was definitely taken by it.

"This thing is only thirty bucks?" I asked.

"Looks like it," Ethan said.

"I'm getting it."

"You're what?"

"You don't like it?"

"I'm just shocked that you like it," he said.

"Well, I do. It's soft. It's longer than a lot of the scarves I have, which is nice. And the design really is pretty."

"Then by all means, get it," he said.

I walked up to the cash register and laid it down for the smiling woman behind the counter, but then I froze. She rang it up and rattled off the price, but I was stuck between a rock and a hard place. I didn't quite have enough cash on me because of my little tantrum back in D.C., and I couldn't use my credit cards while I was in captivity.

"Actually, I think maybe—"

"Here, allow me."

Ethan's voice took me by surprise as he reached over my shoulder. I watched him hand the woman a card before she rang up the scarf. Then, she stuck it in a bag and handed it to me. I turned and looked at Ethan, studying the grin spreading across his cheeks.

"You didn't have to do that," I said.

"You're welcome," he said.

I snickered and shook my head as a smile crossed my face.

"Thank you, Ethan."

"You're welcome, Diana. Now come on. It's lunch time."

We backtracked and made our way to the cafe like we promised. Miss Ethel came up to us and insisted we have a slice of pie before we ordered anything else. And when I dug into that homemade chocolate mousse, I moaned in appreciation. It was so good, and the chocolate melted on the tip of my tongue. The merengue was a perfect consistency and even the crust of the pie had a cinnamon sweetness to it. I hummed my gratitude for it. And with each sound that left my lips, Miss Ethel beamed with more pride than I'd ever seen on any one human's face.

But I was painfully aware of how Ethan was staring at me.

I watched him lick his lips in between the bites of his pie he took. But something told me he wasn't licking his lips to catch bits of pie that had been left behind. My eyes connected with his and I felt myself growing wet at the heat permeating his gaze. I took another bite of my pie, making a show of wrapping my lips around it. I hummed and groaned at the taste, watching as Ethan's eyes fell to the performance I gave him.

Then, his eyes looked up over my shoulder and he groaned in frustration.

"Fancy seeing the two of you here."

Rebecca's voice hit my ears and I watched Ethan sigh.

"Hey there, Mom," he said.

"Are you going to scoot over for your mother? Or shall I sit by Miss Diana?" she asked.

"You're more than welcome to sit by me anytime," I said, grinning.

"See? That is how you treat your mother. Diana, I'd love to sit by you."

I slid over and let her fall into the booth next to me while Ethan stared at her. I could tell he was annoyed by her presence, and I didn't understand why. Didn't he know how lucky he was? I'd give anything to share something like this with my mother.

"What are you doing here, Mom?" Ethan asked.

"Well, I stopped by the house to make lunch for you guys and Liam said you two were in town. I was out walking, saw you two in here, and figured I'd stop in," Rebecca said.

"I'm glad you did," I said, smiling.

"At least someone's happy to see me," she said.

"You're being a little stalkerish, Mom," Ethan said.

"I think it's endearing, honestly. I'd give anything for my mother to be alive so she could do something like that," I said.

The words flew out before I could catch them and the entire table fell silent. I felt like an idiot, and my cheeks flushed with embarrassment.

"I mean, I live downtown here, anyway. I moved myself into a slightly smaller space after my husband died, Diana. So, it wasn't hard finding the two of you. After all, this is Ethan's favorite place to come eat when he's in town," she said.

"I'm so sorry for your loss," I said.

"After my husband passed, the estate felt too big. Too lonely out there on that piece of property. Downsizing was the right move for me. It put me in the heart of a city I've loved all my life. It keeps me warm at night now. Plus, I'm closer to all the action and the drama."

"Oh yeah, all the nightlife action. Like the hoedown on 51st that lasts until a whopping eleven o'clock at night," Ethan said.

He tossed me a playful wink and I had to hold back a laugh.

"It might not be exciting for you, but is it exciting for me," Rebecca said.

"Then, that's all that matters," I said.

"See? Why can't you treat your mother like that?" she asked.

"Because she constantly insists on meddling in things and breaking rules to keep her safe," Ethan said.

"Pish posh. You sound like your father," she said.

"I'll take that as a compliment," he said.

I giggled at their interaction while watching the way they looked at one another. It was clear Rebecca loved her son more than anything on this planet, and it was very clear Ethan adored his mother. Their playful relationship made me insanely jealous of what the two of them shared. I'd never know that type of relationship with either of my parents. Ethan's eyes caught my stare and he winked at me again. A gesture that sent my stomach exploding with butterflies.

I enjoyed playful Ethan. I enjoyed familial Ethan. Hell, I enjoyed Ethan, in general. And I was happy to get to spend the day with him in town. No matter what kind of town it was.

Chapter 15

Ethan

I couldn't believe my mother sometimes. I knew exactly what she was doing. And despite her meddling, I knew nothing could affect my mood. I was having a good time showing Diana around my hometown, and not even my meddling mother who was trying to hook us up could get in the way of that.

If only she knew the things we had already done.

Honestly, I was shocked by the way Diana was so taken with Abington. I thought for sure she'd be disappointed at the small town and the little it had to offer her in terms of what she was used to. Honestly, on the drive over, I had braced myself for her brat-like ways. I had prepared myself for a meltdown or for her to try and make a break for it. But instead, we'd had a lovely time. We walked around, she listened as I told her about the history of the town. And surprisingly, she listened and absorbed it all. She even found herself something she really wanted to purchase and I was able to buy it for her.

For some reason, that really topped out the day for me.

"So, what are the two of you getting into next?" my mother asked.

"I figured lunch was a good way to round out the day before we headed back to the house," I said.

"Please tell me you took Diana to our famous square with the lovely fountain," my mother said.

"Fountain? What fountain?" Diana asked.

"You didn't take her to the fountain?" my mother asked.

"No, we hadn't made it that far down," Ethan said.

"Could we go?" Diana asked.

101

Her eyes were wide with curiosity and that shocked me even more. She wanted to stay out in town? She wanted to keep walking around all of the thrift shops and boutiques? This wasn't like the Diana I had come to know at all, and it intrigued me. Though with the way my mother was talking, it almost sounded as if she was going to tag along with us.

"Come on. I'll show it to you, Diana. Ethan can sit here like a bump on a log," my mother said playfully.

Great. My mother was coming along.

"I'll get lunch. The two of you wait for me outside," I said.

"He's such a good boy. I trained him right," my mother said.

She and Diana shared a giggle as my mother linked her arm with Diana's and guided her out the front door.

What the hell had I just gotten myself into?

I paid for our lunch, then walked between the two of them as we headed to the fountain. It wasn't much. The square was a patch of land at the end of the fourteen-block stretch that was paved and decorated. It had a splash fountain the kids of the town could run around in during the summer months and it had a covered stage that sat off towards the back where weekly outdoor concerts took place throughout the year. Diana and my mother pulled away from me, talking and getting to know one another. And for a split second, I thought I saw a genuine smile cross Diana's face.

Relaxed. Rested. And genuine.

"Abingdon really is a darling town," Diana said.

"Well, I'm glad you like our little corner of the world," my mother said.

My heart swelled with pride at hearing those words come from Diana. I liked that she liked the town. I'd always loved it, despite how little I got back to visit. We walked around the square and Diana took in a few kids running through the fountain and I saw a sparkle in her eye. She looked at the children almost endearingly, and I could've sworn her eyes unfocused there for a second.

Like she was ripped into a dream-like state.

"Have you been into our little jewelry shop?" my mother asked.

"There's a jewelry shop around here?" Diana asked.

"There is. It's owned by a middle-aged couple in the area. They make all of their own pieces."

"Wait, all of them?"

"All of them. Handcrafted in the back of their store. Some on a daily basis," my mother said.

"Can we go?" Diana asked.

She looked back at me with an eagerness I'd never be able to disappoint.

"Of course we can. Lead the way, Mom," I said.

We slipped into the store up the block and I watched as Diana's eyes scoured the walls. She took in all the glittering loose diamonds before walking over to the glass cases. Her fingertips ran over the tops of them and I watched the gemstones and diamonds reflected in her amber gaze. She was entranced by all of it. But not in a selfish way. It was as if I was seeing an entirely new person emerging from her, and it kept me on my toes.

"Could I try that necklace on?" Diana asked.

One of the attendants came around and unlocked the case before bringing out the display.

She had better taste than I would have expected. I thought she would have gravitated to the largest and most expensive pieces in the store. But instead, I watched as she tried on a delicate diamond necklace. Each diamond was accented with a small, ocean-washed pearl, and it glistened against her olive skin. Her eyes sparkled with delight. A healthy flush rose against her cheeks. She brought the necklace away from her skin, then placed it back on the velvet and stroked it softly with her fingers.

"It suits you," the store clerk said.

"Thank you for letting me try it on," Diana said.

I watched the clerk put it back while Diana traveled the store some more. She didn't spare a thought to purchasing it, nor did she look back at me to see if I could get it for her. Especially since I had set the precedence. And in that moment, I decided I was going to get it for her. The way her eyes sparkled when she looked at it in the mirror indicated a happiness that I hadn't seen in her before.

But before I could track down the clerk, my phone buzzed against my hip.

"This is Ethan," I said.

"Stark. It's Liam. I've got news from Logan in D.C. Can you get back to the estate?"

"That bad?"

"Don't want to discuss this on the wire, no."

"Sure. Yeah. I can make it back to the estate," I said.

"I've got one of the guys already heading to the downtown area. If Diana wants to stay out, he can take over guarding her while you get back."

I saw something black move in my vision and I turned my head towards the front door of the store. I watched Granger come in and stand in the corner, looming over all of us. Sometimes, I forgot how efficient Liam was because I was too focused on reminding him to keep his dick in check.

And I felt Diana's gaze on me as her face fell in my peripheral vision.

"I'll be back soon," I said.

"Talk then," Liam said.

"Is everything okay, sweetheart?" my mother asked.

Diana stayed over in her corner, watching the scene but not interjecting herself into it. She looked almost sad, and when her gaze turned to the man at the door her stoic stare took over. She wasn't happy, and I didn't blame her.

I wasn't happy about leaving, either.

"I have to go for a little bit. Work," I said.

"Well, don't work yourself too hard, okay?" my mother asked.

"I'll try not to. But the man at the door is going to keep you and Diana company until I get back or you two get home, okay?"

"Of course. I know how it goes. I'll make sure Diana stays safe."

"No, Mom. Not your job. That's his job. You just stay alert and keep yourself safe."

I bent down and kissed her cheek before I made my way for the door. The disappointment that washed over Diana's face punched me in my gut. But I forced myself to push past it. I walked out on the sidewalk and ran my ass back to my SUV, then hopped in and got myself back to the estate. Her safety was paramount, and I wouldn't allow anything to compromise that.

Not even her own wishes.

Annoyance filled my veins as I grew closer to my childhood home. I didn't want my day with Diana to be interrupted. I wanted to spend the entire day at her side, exploring my hometown with her and watching this new woman blossom before my eyes.

I slammed my car into park and pushed my way through the front door, feeling my hot-headed temper rise up my throat.

"Liam. Report. Now," I barked.

"Diana must've thrown a diva-scale tantrum today," he said, grinning.

I glared at him as I rounded my way into the office and it shut him up. Then, he shrugged and took over the debriefing.

"Senator Logan received another package, but this one was dropped off at the damn door of his hotel room," he said.

"How the hell is that even possible? No one knew where he was staying except us," I said.

"Well, the perp figured it out. We've been moving his location every other day, following standard protocols put in place. Mason's making sure they aren't followed, and the room is swept for bugs every time. They take a circuitous route, the senator has a curfew, and he takes all of his meals in his room where it's first tested for poisonous agents."

"Do you have a picture of the package?" I asked.

Liam pulled up pictures on his phone and handed it over to me. And the contents made my stomach roll. Inside of the black box were two white rabbits. One of them larger, one of them smaller. Both of them with severed heads. This box also contained a note that was written in much the same manner as the first.

"And before you ask, yes. That's the rabbit's blood used to write that note," Liam said.

"Great," I said flatly.

You can try to hop away, little bunnies, but you can't escape your crimes. Or your punishment.

Anger surged through me. How dare someone threaten Diana's life? I felt my possessiveness blanket me and I was helpless to stop it. Every fiber of my being filled with a need to protect her, and I was powerless to push the feeling away.

I had to let it swallow me. I had no other choice.

"I want that damn box sent to the lab immediately. I want fucking clues, and if our lab can't get them then you let them know we're finding another damn lab to pair up with. It's time to catch this son of a bitch. This has gone on long enough," I said.

"On it. I'll let the lab know," Liam said.

"Keep me updated every fucking step of the way. Whenever you hear from that lab, I want your first call to be to me."

"Not to the police?"

"No. I'm first. They're second. Got it?" I asked.

"Loud and clear, Ethan."

I wasn't letting this asshole get away with this a second longer. I was going to put my hands on this man before he was turned over to the police. And when I did, I was going to let him know that he didn't fuck with my clients. That he didn't fuck with me.

And that he sure as hell didn't fuck with Diana.

Chapter 16

Diana

"You know, Ethan was first in his class in college," Rebecca said.

"He was valedictorian?" I asked.

"He was. Graduated college early and joined the military straight out of school."

"That's incredible. Did he enjoy the military?"

"Not as much as his father, I think. He only re-enlisted once. But when he decided not to make the military a career, he began one of the most successful security businesses in the country."

"I can tell you're very proud of him," I said.

"He's a good man. He's got his quirks like everyone else, but I raised a fine boy. Any woman would be lucky to have him."

I grinned as the two of us strolled down the sidewalk with Mr. Black Suit looming behind us.

"So, what about you?"

"What about me?" I asked.

"What do you do with your life when you aren't being cooped up by my son?"

I giggled and shook my head at her obvious motives.

"Well, I went to college as well. Got a Bachelor's in Business that has been practically useless."

"That doesn't sound so useless. What did you want to do with it?" Rebecca asked.

"I don't know. I still don't. I chose Business because it was easy."

"A Business degree was easy for you."

"Yeah. It was. The budgets and the business plans and the strategic classes. I fell asleep in most of them and still ended up with A's and B's."

"It takes an intelligent woman to do something like that. My son is intelligent like that as well."

"He strikes me as such, yes."

"Did you ever date while you were sleeping through classes in college?" she asked.

I threw my head back and laughed as we started down a side street littered with old brick buildings.

"No, I didn't. Not seriously, anyway. I was asked out on dates, and I went on some, but it was all mostly for fun," I said.

"What about now? Are you dating anyone?"

"I am not," I said, grinning.

"What do you look for in someone you are dating?"

I shook my head and smiled down at the sidewalk as Rebecca led me into one of the buildings.

"Where are we going?" I asked.

"Oh, this is an art gallery. The only one Abingdon has, actually. I know the owner," she said.

"I love art galleries. But I've never enjoyed going into them alone."

"Because they aren't meant to be enjoyed alone."

I turned around at the sound of the unfamiliar voice and saw a tall man approaching us. He was very tall. Easily a foot above me. He had dark blonde hair that was swept off to the side and dark green eyes that matched the tie he was wearing. His smile was broad. Kind. Gentle.

"Diana, this is the owner of the gallery. Oliver Benson," Rebecca said.

"But most people call me Ollie," he said.

He extended his hand and I took it, watching as his palm dwarfed mine. His touch was kind and soft.

The exact opposite of Ethan's.

"It's nice to meet you. I'm Diana," I said.

"And I know everything I already need to know about you if Rebecca has taken a liking to you," he said.

"Oliver here made his mint in the technological sector. Retired at thirty-three years of age, moved to Abingdon, and opened up this gallery for all of us small-town folk to enjoy," Rebecca said.

"That's an incredible accomplishment. Congratulations," I said.

"I wanted to find a place that moved at a slower pace than what I was used to. I made my billions, and I didn't want it to fly from my pocket as quickly as I had made it. From the second I stepped into Abingdon, I knew it was the place for me. Now, I dedicate my time to purchasing art and bringing it here for the enrichment of a town that has taken me in as one of their own," he said.

"Now come here. You've gone too long without giving me a hug, Oliver," Rebecca said.

I watched the tall man bend down and hug Rebecca and I stepped away from both of them. It was clear he was beloved in the community, so I let them talk while I walked around the gallery. There were some incredible paintings on the walls. Some looked old. As if they had been passed down. Others looked commissioned. Bright and colorful and wild. There were sculptures that permeated the corners and ornate wrought-iron blacksmithy pieces that hung along the tops of the walls where the crown-molding would have been.

The place was spectacular.

Standing in front of a beautiful piece that had bright yellows and greens and oranges splattered all over a stark black background, I couldn't stop looking at it. All of the splatters somehow swirled into one another, and at the center of the entire piece was—well, something that sort of resembled a vagina.

"What do you see?" Oliver asked.

I jumped at his smooth voice in my ear before my eyes turned back to the painting.

"Honestly? I see this as a sort of praise piece for the female form," I said.

I heard Ollie snicker and I turned my gaze up to him.

"What?" I asked.

"You're the first person I've come across that hit the nail on the head the first time," he said.

"So, this is what I think it is."

"It certainly is."

"It's a very interesting piece, that's for certain. Though I'm not shocked it's still hanging on your wall."

"Why is that?" he asked.

"It's a small town. Small towns usually have conservative values. I'm sure not many people want a painted vagina hanging on their wall."

Ollie chuckled and the sound was soothing. Which was a reaction I hadn't expected from myself.

"I've actually had five offers on it. Four of them from elderly couples in the area."

"No you haven't," I said.

"I really have," he said.

"Seriously? Old people around here want this on their wall?" I asked.

"I mean, if they think it's really a piece of fruit in the middle, who am I to correct them? Art is, after all, subjective."

I threw my head back and laughed before shaking my head.

"Oh, what I wouldn't give to be a fly on the wall when one of those children told their parents they had a vagina hanging on their wall," I said.

"I don't think I've ever heard the casual use of 'vagina' worked into a conversation with such a beautiful woman in my entire life."

My lips parted in shock as an embarrassed flush crossed my cheeks.

"Um—where did Rebecca go?" I asked.

"She went to the bathroom. She'll be back soon, I promise," he said.

"Okay."

"So, what brings you to our small town?"

"Uh—just visiting the Stark family for a little bit."

"Don't tell me Ethan finally took enough time off to snag a beautiful girlfriend. I don't think he'd appreciate me flirting with his woman."

"First off, I would never be anyone's property," I said.

"Oh, never. I wouldn't even dream it," Ollie said.

"And secondly, no. Ethan is working as we speak. I'm out spending the day with Rebecca. Well, part of the day. I was out with Ethan earlier before work pulled him away. And I'm not his girlfriend. Wait, how do you know Ethan?"

I looked up at Ollie and the grin on his face grew bigger. His dark green eyes sparkled with delight and I felt myself being pinned by his gaze. Heat ripped up the nape of my neck as his eyes comfortably stared into mine.

"I'm glad to hear that," Ollie said.

"Um... which part?" I asked.

I'd never been this flustered with a man before. Ollie was easy on the eyes. Good-looking as hell. And apparently, filthy rich. And it was true. I wasn't Ethan's girlfriend. But maybe I wanted to be? We'd had such a wonderful time that morning out in the town, and I was sorely disappointed when he had to leave and get back to the house. But every time I turned around, Ethan was throwing mixed signals. One minute he was leading me into a secret garden and telling me how beautiful I was and the next minute he was making any moves he could to get out of a room I was in. I felt more confused than ever as Ollie drew closer, and I felt his body heat radiating against my skin.

"This piece was actually done by a local woman. She's older as well, if you can believe it," he said.

"You mean the vagina piece?" I asked.

"Mhm. The intimate portrait of a woman's physique."

I melted at the way he phrased that.

"I commissioned it when I saw another one of her works. She sits on the corner and paints on the weekends, and I was taken by her style. She took up painting when her wife passed."

"Her wife?" I asked.

"Believe it or not, many people in this town are a lot more open-minded than you give them credit for."

I nodded my head as I listened to him ramble on about the artist. The painting. The background story of it all and how it came to fruition. Ollie was knowledgeable and funny, making me giggle as his lips migrated closer and closer to my ear. Everything about him screamed intimate. Romantic. Commanding, but in a softer aspect.

If it wasn't for my confusion regarding Ethan, I'd be all over him.

"Well, it looks like the two of you are getting along," Rebecca said.

I felt Ollie lean up from my shoulder before I turned and greeted with Ethan's mother with a smile.

"Are you all right, Diana? You look a little flushed," she said.

I saw Ollie grin out of the corner of my eye and I cleared my throat.

"Just a little thirsty, I think," I said.

"Well, it is getting to be close to dinner time. Maybe we should slip in somewhere and get you something," Rebecca said.

"Have the two of you tried that new Indian restaurant that opened up across the street?" Ollie asked.

"No, but I've been meaning to try it. Didn't it just open up last week?" Rebecca asked.

"It did. You'll have to let me know how you like the food," Ollie said.

"Why? Do you enjoy it?" I asked.

"Well, that and I own it," he said, smiling.

"You crazy lunatic! You didn't open that restaurant," Rebecca said.

My lips parted in shock as Ollie's eyes met mine.

"I'd love to join the two of you for dinner, if it isn't too much trouble. It'll give me a first-hand perspective on the customer experience," he said.

My eyes darted over to Rebecca and I found her smiling broadly.

"We'd enjoy that greatly. But trust me, if I don't like it, I will let you know," she said.

"It's why I've always valued your opinion, Rebecca," Ollie said.

The three of us walked across the street to the Indian restaurant and we were promptly seated. Ollie ordered for the three of us, proclaiming that he thought they were the three best dishes on the menu. And he was right. From the second the food came out, it looked and smelled fabulous. But when I put my first bite of spicy chicken curry between my lips, I practically melted into my chair.

"Oh. My. Gosh," I said.

"You like?" Ollie asked.

"Oliver, this is incredible," Rebecca said.

"Not too much spice? Enough chicken for the rice?" he asked.

"It's perfect," I said.

His eyes whipped over to mine and the smile he gave me practically curled my damn toes.

"I'm glad you like it," he said.

"Mm, you should tell Diana that story," Rebecca said.

"What story?" I asked.

I watched Ollie shake his head before he took a sip of his water.

"I have this story I tell people about a code battle between some of the software nerds back when I was in the tech industry. Rebecca loves the way I tell it," he said.

"Will you tell it to me?" I asked.

"If you'd like to hear it."

"I really, really would."

I had no idea what the hell the man was talking about. He was talking about coders and bugs and C++ and all sorts of nonsense I didn't understand. He talked about finding loopholes for money, whatever that meant. Patching up software. Races until dawn. All sorts of insane shit I had a hard time deciphering. But the passion with which he spoke was entrancing. He had a lot to say and he had no problem saying it. He was confident. Poised. A real snake charmer. I laughed along with Rebecca during his stories, taken by the way he told them. I spun myself so deep into his web, actually, that I didn't notice when he slipped his arm against the small of my back and pulled me closer to his side.

However, Rebecca noticed.

"Ethan! There you are, sweetheart. It's about time you joined us. Can you let this man to go have some dinner now? He won't sit down and eat with us," she said.

I whipped my head over towards him and watched the black-suited man looming around us trade places with Ethan, who didn't look happy at all. His face was a thundercloud and I swallowed as he approached our booth. I felt Ollie's hand grip my waist tighter and I was suddenly very uncomfortable. I shook him off and he immediately read my body language, removing his hand and putting a bit of space between us.

Just like a gentleman.

In any other world, I would have hopped on Ollie and ridden his face off into the sunset. But with Ethan glaring at me the way he was with a staunch look of anger in his face, the only thing I felt was guilt. An overwhelming sense of guilt.

Even though I had no reason to feel that way.

Chapter 17

Ethan

W hat the fuck was Ollie doing with his arm around Diana? The second I walked into that restaurant, my vision dripped red. White hot jealousy snagged my mind. I stalked over to them, my fists clenched at my sides as Ollie's eyes caught mine. He smiled at me. Just—smiled. Like he knew what he was doing. Like he knew Diana was mine and he didn't give a shit about it. I saw Diana shake him off. I saw her scoot over as Ollie removed his hand from her waist. Good. Served him right.

No one touched that waist but me.

"Ethan! There you are, sweetheart. It's about time you joined us. Can you let this man to go have some dinner now? He won't sit down and eat with us," my mother said.

I looked at the man standing near the booth and nodded my head. It was time for him to go. In fact, it was time for all of us to go.

"Will you sit and eat with us?" Diana asked.

My eyes fell to hers before I reached around and pulled out my wallet.

"No. I'll eat back at the estate. We need to return anyway. Everyone's been out long enough," I said.

"No, no, no. Allow me. I promised the girls a nice dinner, so I'll pay for it," Ollie said.

"Your money isn't necessary, Oliver," I said.

"Save yours, Ethan. Trust me. I've got it," he said.

I went to respond, but my mother slid from the booth and quickly stood to her feet. She put her arm around me and pulled me away, guiding me from Diana's form. I looked back and saw Ollie grinning at me while Diana gave me an inquisitive stare. He placed his card into the plate for the check and it was carried off, and all the while my mother was trying to get me alone to chastise me for something.

"Ethan, bad manners are for bad boys and I know I didn't raise one."

My eyes dropped to my mother and I opened my mouth to say something, but she narrowed her eyes at me. I drew in a deep breath to try and keep my raging emotions under control. The next time I had to leave anywhere, Diana was coming with me. None of this bullshit of my mother escorting her around. How the hell had they wound up at dinner with Ollie Benson anyway?

I nodded my head to my mom, knowing I couldn't fight with her. I watched the waitress brush by us with the paid check, and I followed her steps until she was back with Diana and Oliver. I trained my ears onto their conversation. I watched that man smile at her. He reached for his card and slid it back into his wallet, then allowed his stare to bounce off her chest a little longer than I would have wanted.

"I really need to get going," Diana said.

"That's fine. I understand. Maybe you'll pop back into the gallery sometime?" Ollie asked.

The art gallery. Of course. My mother loved that place.

"That sounds like fun, sure," Diana said.

"Well, if you'd like, you could give me your number and I can let you know when I get some new pieces in from that artist you seemed so entranced with."

I watched Diana blush and every single part of me wanted to tear into Ollie at that very moment.

"Well, I don't have my phone at the moment," Diana said.

"No phone? Why in the world not?" Ollie asked incredulously.

"I just don't have it on me right now."

"Are you doing it for a reason? Less screen time? Spending more time with those you care for?"

"Sorry, but we have to get going. Diana?" I asked.

Her eyes panned over to mine and I knew I didn't look sorry. Not in the least. I also didn't give a fuck what I looked like. Ollie was digging for information he wasn't privy to, and that didn't sit well with me. I strode over to Diana and wrapped my hand around her arm, then tugged her from the booth and guided her towards the door. Thank hell the SUV was sitting right there on the curb. I quickly piled her into the passenger's seat before I wrapped around, then climbed behind the wheel of the car.

I looked up just in time to see my mother come in to give me a kiss on the cheek, then she closed my SUV door and started off towards her apartment.

I peeled away from the curb as quickly as I could, my mind running away with me. Of course, Diana flocked right to Ollie. Of course, she would fawn over him. He was a charming billionaire. The only one in town. He had money. Fame. Passion. Swoon-like features. Maybe I had been wrong about Diana all along. Maybe she was only interested in men with money. Those who could provide her with a luxurious lifestyle. I mean, I had tons of money. Plenty of it. I could buy myself an island, retire right now, build a damn village on it, and keep it up for four entire lifetimes. Easily. Not a problem in the world. But I didn't have Ollie's idle rich flare. I didn't boast and flaunt my wealth. I didn't drape myself in expensive fabrics and use my riches as a way to get women underneath the crook of my damn arm.

Was that the kind of man Diana wanted?

I ground my teeth. I white-knuckled the steering wheel of my car. I bit down onto my tongue so hard it caused me to growl. I bit back jealous words that were dancing on the tip of my tongue. Threatening to spill over and fill the SUV with nothing but heated rage.

And as each mile ticked on, I found my resolve dwindling.

"So, you think you're going to take Ollie up on his offer?" I asked.

I felt Diana's eyes pan over to me before she furrowed her brow.

"What?" she asked.

"You know. Giving him your number. Think you might take him up on it?"

"Wouldn't make sense since I can't use my phone. You told me to stay off it," she said, confused.

I shook my head as my molars released the inside of my cheek.

"You could give him your number to call after all of this is over," I said.

Glancing over at Diana, I saw her narrow those beautiful eyes of hers at me.

"Should I give Ollie my number?" she asked.

"Do you want to?" I asked.

I watched her close her eyes as her head leaned back into the passenger's seat of the SUV. I heard her draw in a deep breath as her beautiful eyes fluttered open, then she languidly crossed one leg over the other. She clasped her hands in her lap, as if she was about to have some sort of frank conversation with someone.

Shit.

What had I just opened up?

"Well, I could. He's attractive. Rich. Retired, except for the gallery. So he'd have a lot of free time on his hands. A lot of time to spend with me. He doesn't seem like the type of man that would push me away. Or be ashamed of me. So, that would be a nice change of pace."

Change of pace? What the fuck did that mean?

"Those are all decent points, I guess," I said.

"He's also intelligent. Knowledgeable about art. I like that about him."

"Are you knowledgeable about art?"

"The interpretation of art is in the eye of the beholder," she said.

"Sounds like the two of you would be a good match, then," I said flatly.

"Then maybe I should look him up once I'm allowed to have a life again."

Chapter 18

Diana

The car fell silent again as we drove straight to the estate. The entire time, I couldn't figure out what the hell had gotten into Ethan. He came back from the estate all pissed off and wound up, then he just yanked me out of that booth like it was nothing. I was tired of being yanked around. Manhandled without any of the pleasures that came along with it. I wasn't someone's rag doll. I wasn't anyone's toy. And I was beginning to resent Ethan for the way he treated me in those moments of heated emotion. And what was with the questions about Ollie? Wanting to know if I'd give him my cell number that I couldn't even use anyway? Why the hell did he care?

If I didn't know any better, I'd think Ethan was jealous.

But, Ethan didn't get jealous, did he? I mean, what did he have to be jealous about? I was his dirty little secret. His little common whore. He was a professional working a job, and he never ceased to remind me of that every time he was disgusted with what we did together in my garden. So, why the hell was he acting like a pissy little bitch all of a sudden?

I was growing tired of his mood swings and his mixed signals.

We pulled up to the estate and once he'd parked the SUV, I slammed out of the vehicle. I didn't want to be cooped up with him a second longer. Ethan rushed to get to my side and opened up the front door for me, but I brushed past him and headed straight for the stairs. I took them as quickly as I could, not looking back even though I felt Ethan's gaze hot on my trail. I slid into my room and closed the door behind me. I even thought about locking it.

But I figured he'd probably have a key to the damn thing. So, no point in that.

There was no reason to indulge Ethan and his mood. At least, there was no reason for me to. We weren't together and he had no reason to be acting the way he was. I closed my eyes and sank my back against the door as my mind swirled. Things had been so good this morning. We had fun. We played dress up. He bought me a beautiful scarf. Took me out for lunch. His playful side came out and it mesmerized me. Filled me with a happiness I hadn't felt in a long time.

What changed all that?

It didn't matter. In the end, none of it did. I pulled off my clothes and slipped into my nightgown, then tried to relax a little bit in bed. I sank down into the plush covers and closed my eyes, trying to go to bed early. Trying to get some rest. To calm my mind. But no matter what I did and no matter how hard I tried, I couldn't get myself to go to sleep.

My mind wouldn't stop racing, and I was still annoyed with the way Ethan had treated me. I threw the covers off of me as my eyes fell to the digital clock on the nightstand. A quarter after midnight. Great. Another sleepless night ahead of me in the darkness of the country with nothing but the crickets to keep me company. Sounded fabulous.

Not.

Pulling my silken robe over my white silk nightgown, I quietly opened my door. I didn't want to wake anyone up. In fact, what I really wanted was to be alone. I'd been surrounded by people intent on hovering over me for weeks and I was growing tired of it. Tired of everyone being in my business and clocking my every move. I headed out into the hallway, my footsteps as silent as I could make them. I clutched my silken robe tightly around my body, then tied off the strings around my waist.

Maybe a bit of exploring would help wind down my mind.

My eyes cased the walls of the hallway as I dipped down a small corridor. At the end of it was a set of French double doors with curtains that caught the moonlight just right. I walked down the hallway and put my hands on the doorknobs, then quietly opened them. I sighed at the sight. A private balcony with a railing that overlooked the whole backyard of the estate.

I walked out onto the balcony and felt the cool summer breeze against my face. The moon cast a glow over my face as the cacophony of sounds hit my ears. Insects and frogs. Birds and the rustling of leaves. The fluttering of grass while the wind kicked up. In some cases, I could've sworn I heard the stars twinkling for me. I gazed out among the massive trees that lined the Stark estate. Nothing but nature for miles.

So different than what I was used to in the city.

"Why are you out here?"

I ground my teeth at the sound of Ethan's voice. Feeling him approach me, his body heat was radiating against my shoulder as he walked over to stand beside me. Fuck. I couldn't get one moment's peace in this damn place. I looked over at him as my eyes drifted over his body. He wore nothing but sweatpants and a black t-shirt and his hair was mussed from lying in bed. I turned my gaze back out into the night. Out into the beauty of the country I was surrounded with as my mind tried to block him out.

What the hell was she doing out here? Wait, what was he doing out here?

"I could ask you the same question," I said.

"I heard the doors open and wondered what you were doing," Ethan said.

I crossed my arms over my chest as a frown took over my face. I was really growing tired of how hot and cold Ethan was running. One minute he was yanking me from a booth with a rough touch any real man would have regarded as inappropriate, then the next minute he was concerned about my well-being.

Well, if he wanted to talk, we would talk. I wanted answers anyway.

"Why do you care what I'm doing?" I asked.

His silence to my question pissed me off.

"Why are you always tracking my movements?" I asked.

I turned my gaze over to him and he looked at me as if I had asked the stupidest question on the face of the planet.

"I'm being paid to keep tabs on you, Diana. That's why I'm tracking your movements."

"You didn't have to track me down at the restaurant. One of your men was with me. If you wanted me to come back, all you had to do was call him and he would've gladly escorted me back to the estate, despite my insistence on staying for the rest of dinner. So, I'll ask you again. Why are you tracking my movements even when you don't have to?"

His eyes locked onto mine, but he didn't answer my question. I wasn't allowing him to leave without answering me.

"You didn't have to come out onto this porch and ask what I was doing out here. All you had to do was peek out and make sure I wasn't launching myself over the balcony and making a break for the woods. Yet here you are, standing beside me, asking me what I'm doing with my time. After you yanked me out of that booth so hard my arm still hurts."

I watched his face falter before his eyes fell to my upper arm.

"Yeah. Yanking me around hurts, asshole," I said.

"I didn't mean to hurt you."

"Well, you did. Like my father did. Does. All the time. But none of that matters. What matters is that you will answer my question. I know there's something more going on here. Something more going on between us. We had a fantastic time out this morning, Ethan. It was wonderful. All of it. Every second with you was incredible. Then you had to leave, and when you come back you were in a foul mood from the minute you walked into the restaurant. What happened?"

I watched him draw in a deep breath before he turned his eyes out onto his estate.

"What happened, Ethan?" I asked.

"I don't want to bother you with the details of the case," he said.

"I don't enjoy being treated like a child and kept in the dark. If this has something to do with me and my safety, I deserve to know it. My father might not want to obey that premise, but I expect you to."

He glanced over at me as his hands wrapped around the wrought iron railing of the balcony. I was done, and if he didn't want to give me answers and be straight with me, then whatever the fuck this was we were doing with one another was also done.

I no longer enjoyed his games.

"Your father got another package with another threatening letter," he said.

"That's why you were so pissy?" I asked.

He nodded before he rose up from the balcony, his eyes panning over to mine. His icy gaze darkened as he loomed over me, his shadow encompassing the moonlight drenching my features. I gripped onto the wrought iron railing to keep myself steady. I already felt my knees giving way underneath his stare. His eyes intensified, mesmerizing me and holding me in its own tight grasp.

Then, he uttered words I never thought I'd hear him say.

"That was why I was pissy, yes. That, and seeing that fucker Ollie with his arm wrapped around you."

Chapter 19

Ethan

Diana's eyes widened as the moon was reflected in her amber stare. There was no going back. If she wanted answers, I'd give them to her. In the pit of my gut, I knew she deserved them. But I didn't know what that would mean for any of this going forward. But, it didn't matter. Not in the long run, anyway. I'd seen a change in Diana. Despite the interactions I witnessed between her and Ollie, I had watched her change. I'd watched her settle down. I watched her take in the beauty of this place and actually enjoy it, despite her city-girl ways.

I wanted to give her the answers she sought.

"Ollie?" she asked.

"Yes. Ollie. I didn't like his hands on you. Period."

I watched her lips turn into a frown even though her pupils were blown wide with want for me.

"I'm still technically single, Ethan."

My own lips turned down at her rebuttal.

"Besides, if you hadn't left, there wouldn't have been any danger from the handsome billionaire art dealer for you to deal with," she said.

"I had work to do, Diana!"

I felt myself pop as I reached out and grabbed her arms.

"I had work to do! I have to protect you, Diana. Don't you get that?"

She was trying to pull away from me, but I wouldn't release her. I wouldn't let go. She had to understand. I had to get it through her thick skull that I didn't leave her because I wanted to, but because that was how I protected her. Chasing down this madman was how I was going to make this work. I just needed to shake this case from our backs.

Diana backed into the wrought iron railing and I followed her, my fingers wrapped around her upper arms.

"I'm tired of coming second to your work," she said, breathlessly.

"It's all to keep you safe. Don't you get that?" I asked.

"My father does that to me," she whispered.

My hands slid to her forearms as her body leaned heavily against the railing.

"My father always does that, and now you are."

"It's not the same, Diana. I'm trying to protect your fucking life. What's more important than that?" I asked.

"Actually being present in it, Ethan. Actually being present in my life is more important."

I pulled her up to me and came eye-to-eye with her. I watched her eyes widen as I held her tightly, her skin searing its imprint into my palms. My nostrils flared. My eyes locked onto hers. Diana's gaze danced around in mine as she stood on her tiptoes to keep up with my wants and wishes of her body.

"You're behaving like a brat again," I growled.

"Have you ever thought that maybe I act like that because it's the only way I can get attention from the people I care about the most?" she asked.

Her question gave me pause as her words dawned on my mind. Care about? Was she talking about me?

I felt something inside me pop and I knew she would be the death of me before I could get this case solved.

"Now let me go," Diana said.

I pulled her closer to me as she tried to get out of my grasp.

"Damn it, Ethan, let me g—"

I captured her lips in a searing kiss. A kiss led by the moonlight and finished by the sound of the crickets chirping in the distance. Her hands pressed against my chest and tried to push me away, but I released her arms and sank my hands to her hips. I drew her nearer to me.

I closed the gap between the two of us. Her hands pushed at me to try and separate us, but the second my tongue lapped across her lips I felt her grab my shirt.

And draw me closer.

Her resistance faded and she caved into my palms.

Our tongues connected and everything else disappeared. Ollie. My mother. Dinner. The package. All of it faded away and gave into the night that draped around us. The stars twinkled with delight, clapping and cheering us on as I backed Diana up against the railing again. I pinned her to it. I slid my arms around her back. She threaded her arms around my neck and moaned into my mouth, filling me with a warmth that was unexplainable. My head tilted off to the side. Our teeth clattered together. My hands slid down the smooth globe of her ass, taking in the silken fabric that separated our bodies.

Our foreheads connected and I broke our kiss, taking a second to catch my breath. Then, my face fell to the crook of her neck and I peppered her skin with kisses.

"I don't ever want to see another man touching your perfect body, Diana," I whispered.

"Then stop being so ashamed of me," she said breathlessly.

I felt my heart break as every single part of me shredded to bits. That was what this was all about? This game we played, the dance we perfected. She thought it was because I was ashamed of her. I kissed her shoulder as I bent down, sweeping my arm underneath her knees. I picked her up effortlessly against my body, feeling her cheek come down onto my shoulder. I carried her off the balcony as her tears freely fell. Her arms wrapped around my neck, pulling me closer as I made my way to my room. I walked in and pushed the door closed with my foot, then settled her beautiful form gently onto my four-poster bed.

I smoothed her raven hair away from her eyes before my thumb wiped away the trails of her tears.

"I could never be ashamed of you, Diana."

Her eyebrows ticked with confusion as I climbed onto the bed after her.

"I could never be ashamed of you."

She grabbed at my shirt and pulled me to her, wrapping her beautiful legs around my body. Her hands were everywhere as I devoured her lips. Her tongue. Her essence. She gripped the tendrils of my hair and rolled her hips into me, desperate to have my closer. My hand slid her nightgown and up over her perfect legs, feeling her smooth skin slide against the palm of my hand.

I swallowed every single one of her moans, proud that I could pull them from such a beautiful throat.

We slid from our clothes and fell to the bed, tangled up in one another. My hands explored her body. Massaged her perfect breasts and brought her nipples to puckered peaks. I kissed down her neck, nibbling and sucking on her skin as my hands held her waist. That waist was mine. The only hand imprinted on it should be mine. A swell of possessiveness rose within me, pushing me forward as I slid down her body. I threaded our fingers together as her glistening thighs parted for me, welcoming me against the folds of her pussy.

Blowing a stream of air onto her wet skin, I watched her body jump for my viewing pleasure.

"Tell me what you want," I said.

Diana lifted her head up as I tugged on her arms, arching her chest into the air.

"Damn, Ethan," she breathed.

"Tell me... what you...want, Diana."

The crooks of her legs settled over my shoulders as I kissed each of her thighs with lust.

"I want your tongue against me," she whispered.

I nuzzled my nose against her swollen folds as she bucked nearer to my lips.

"I need your tongue on me," she groaned.

And oh, how her need was music to my ears.

Chapter 20

Diana

His tongue slid into the folds of my pussy and I bit down onto my lower lip to keep from crying out. His hands tugged on my arms, arching my body closer to his face. The passion and possessiveness he displayed took my breath away. The way he commanded our kiss. Forced me to enjoy it, knowing it was what I wanted before I even did. Maybe he really did care about me. But the real question was, did he mean what he said before he kissed me?

Was he really not ashamed of what we were doing together?

My legs jumped and my toes curled as his tongue found my clit. He swirled it around, forcing my hips to buck into his lips. I trembled for him. Shook as stars burst in my vision. Fuck, his tongue was fantastic. He knew exactly where to lick and exactly what to suck on. I bent my legs back. I placed my heels into his shoulders. He moved forward, tilting my pelvis up to him so he could feast on my body.

"Oh shit, Ethan."

He hummed into my pussy as my clit throbbed for him.

"Oh fuck. Lick that pussy. Please. It's been too long. Too long. Too long."

"Mhm," he moaned.

"Give me what I want. Only you can. Please, Ethan. Please don't stop."

"Say that again," he growled.

"Only you can," I whispered.

"Again."

"Only you can give me what I want, Ethan. So please, let me have—oh!"

His tongue flattened over my clit and my hips left the bed. His hands released mine, allowing my fingers to thread through his hair. His hands slid underneath my body and fisted my ass cheeks, bringing my body to his face as if I were the last meal he would ever eat. Juices poured down my ass crack as my toes curled, readying myself for an explosion. Fire coursed through my veins. Electricity seized hold of my mind. I trembled against his face as he licked me deeper, drinking down every drop of me I had for him.

Then, my body released.

"Mhm. Mhm. Mhm, Diana. Oh, yes."

My pleasure had a choke-hold on me as Ethan chanted my name right into my pussy. I bucked against his face, my body jerking and swaying with my ecstasy. I gasped for air. My back hit the bed as he licked every fold of my pussy clean. I felt him rush up my body, my legs folded against his chest as his lips crashed against mine. I licked myself off him as his cock teased my entrance. Pulsing with want for me as my legs remained hanging over his shoulders.

"Get inside me," I whispered against his lips.

And he wasted no time in filling me to the brim.

His hands pinned my wrists down as he fucked me relentlessly. My toes curled and my body laid there helplessly, taking his beautiful assault. His cock dove in and out of my depths as my pussy swallowed him down, pulling juices from my body that dripped down onto his balls. He coated himself in me as my nails dug into the tops of his hands while his mouth swallowed my sounds.

"Ethan. Don't stop. Oh, yes. You feel so good. So good. The best, Ethan."

He growled against my lips before he ripped himself from between my legs. I whimpered at the loss of him as my legs slid from his shoulders. His hands gripped my hips and he turned me over, raising me into the air. Oh, yes. I loved this position. He'd hit me deeper this way than any man had ever gone. I felt his cock slide against my walls and I re-laxed to allow my body to mold with his.

"Holy shit, Diana. So tight for me."

"Only for you. Just for you," I breathed.

He pulled back and slammed against me and I cried out into my pillow. His hand fisted my hair, wrapping his fingers in it and pulling my face back up. I moaned helplessly as he pounded into my body. The sounds of skin slapping skin filled the corners of his room. I smelled my scent all around us. My ass jumped for his viewing pleasure as his hand commanded my movements, tugging on my hair and pulling at me un-til I was upright on all fours.

"You have no idea how beautiful you look right now," he said.

I sighed at his words as his balls began to smack my clit.

"Harder," I groaned.

His hand clamped down into my hair as he slammed into me with a force that left me breathless. My body lurched. The bed rocked. The mattress creaked as juices fell from my pussy and onto the bed below us. His balls slapped my clit as they filled with a need to release, and every time they touched my throbbing mound my thighs trembled. My face fell back to the pillow. My ass stuck up into the air. Ethan released my hair and massaged my ass cheeks, spreading them and tracing his thumb along my puckered hole. I felt him dip his thumb into my drip-ping juices, soaking his skin in me before his thumb came back to my exposed hole. I felt him trace it. Line it. Lube it up with my wetness as my entire body trembled for him.

No man had ever done that before.

No man had ever been inside that hole before.

"Oh, shit Ethan. Mmmm, so good."

He slipped his thumb into my asshole up to his first knuckle and it was enough to drive me over the edge. He was the only man to have ever breached that line with me, and I was ready to give it all over to him.

"Oh, Ethan! Yes! Take me. Have me. I'm all yours. Oh shit. Fill me up. Every hole. Take me. All of me."

I heard him chuckle as he slid in his finger up to the second knuckle. I cried out into the pillow, feeling my legs grow weak underneath me. He wrapped his arm around my waist and held me up to him, fucking me like a dog while his thumb was in my ass. I rocked against him. Sought my end in the confines of his body. His sweat dripped onto my skin and his lips fell against my spine, kissing every divot he found as electricity curled my fingers and toes.

"Cum for me," he grunted.

My eyes rolled into the back of my head as my cheek pressed into the pillow.

"Cum for me and don't hold back," he panted.

"Oh. Shit. Oh. Yes. Oh. Ethan. Oh—"

My body collapsed to the bed and he came right along with me. I felt his cock jumping against my walls as his thumb slowly pumped in and out of my body. Sweat drenched his bed below us. Fluids spilled from my body as I marked him with my scent. His cock filled me until his cum pumped out with my pulses, soaking the bed beneath our hips. His lips pressed to my shoulder. He kissed up the nape of my neck until his lips found my ear. I felt my eyes falling closed and my body giving way to sleep. I felt his body covering me from the darkness. Keeping me safe, even in my most vulnerable moments.

"You're mine," Ethan murmured into my ear.

And I fell asleep in his arms with those two words echoing off the corners of my mind.

The next morning, however, I woke up alone. I turned over and expected to feel Ethan sleeping next to me, but instead his side of the bed was cold. The satin sheet covered my body as I rose up, taking in his room as my hair sat tangled against the crown of my head. Disappointment rushed over my body. I wanted to wake up in his arms. I wanted to spend the morning exploring his skin. I wanted to wake him up with kisses on his cheeks and my leg thrown over his waist and my breasts tucked soundly against the crook of his strong form.

But, we did have to keep up appearances. After all, he had been hired by my father.

It sucked. But it was what it was, and there was nothing I could do about it.

I slid from bed and saw my robe and nightgown neatly folded over a chair in the corner. I smiled as I got up and padded over to get dressed. I clothed myself before I stripped Ethan's bed of its sheets, then tossed them into the hamper in the corner of his room. But before I could get the bed made back up, my stomach rumbled.

I needed some food.

Making my way downstairs, I noticed how brightly the sun was shining. What time was it? I came around the corner into the kitchen and saw the dirty dishes piled up. Then, my eyes migrated over to the microwave. Holy shit, I'd slept until almost eleven in the morning.

It was practically lunch time.

I made myself a fresh cup of coffee to tide me over until lunch. No use eating breakfast now if another meal was right around the corner. I ran my hands through my tangled hair, working out the knots and trying to make myself somewhat presentable in case anyone came around looking for me.

Anyone like Ethan.

I sipped on my coffee and walked around the downstairs, wondering where everyone went. The house seemed eerily quiet, and that worried me a bit. Did Ethan have to go somewhere? Did something else happen? Was my father all right? I walked down the hallway and came to the cracked door of the office where all of the men barricaded themselves throughout the day. And finally, I heard voices.

Of course they were working.

"If the threat comes here, that's a different story," Ethan said.

"Then we need routes of action," Liam said.

"Exactly. Which is why I'm about to run you guys through them. You ready to take notes?" Ethan asked.

I furrowed my brow as I stood at the door, blatantly eavesdropping on the conversation.

"Okay. If the threat shows up here and someone comes through the front door, the basement is our best bet. You get Diana and you get down into the basement and take the cellar to the back exit of the house," Ethan said.

"Got it," Liam said.

"If the threat comes through the back doors, I expect you guys to barricade yourselves around Diana until we can get her to the SUV," Ethan said.

"What if a threat is coming through both doors?" a foreign voice asked.

"You surround Diana and get her into the basement. The cellar exit is concealed from view for a reason. You get Diana down there, you get her through the wine cellar, you get her out that exit, and you get her to the SUV using whatever means necessary. Is that clear?" Ethan asked.

"Crystal," Liam said.

"Since Senator Logan is being stubborn, so long as we're here, the primary goal is keeping Diana safe. No matter what. No matter what we have to do. Diana is the one that matters," Ethan said.

I felt my heart soar at his words. He was putting me first. Emphasizing my safety above all else. I sipped on my coffee as my back fell against the wall, and I ignored the voices that tried to tell me he was being paid to do this. It touched my heart, how adamant he was about keeping me protected. And I didn't want the small voice in my head to ruin it. That voice had almost ruined everything, and I didn't want to give it any more attention.

Closing my eyes, I reveled in the intensity of Ethan's voice as he commanded his men to protect me at all cost. Because whether I liked it or not, I was falling for Ethan Stark.

And there was nothing I could do about it.

Chapter 21

Ethan

My entire body kept tensing and releasing. My muscles ached and my mind kept going blank. I couldn't stop thinking about last night, no matter what kind of work I kept myself buried myself into. I couldn't stop thinking about how Diana had called out for me. How tight she'd felt around my cock. How quickly she had given every inch of herself over to me. I didn't want to stop. I wanted to take every orifice and mark her with me. Making love to Diana was amazing, and my mind wouldn't stop swirling, wondering when I'd get my next chance.

But, sleeping with her was also dangerous. And definitely unprofessional.

What if Senator Logan found out about our relationship? What if it cost us the job? I didn't want to get fired, especially since the threat against them seemed to be ramping up. My job was to protect Diana, and I knew no one else in my sector would do that any better than my team. Better than me. The line we kept toeing and crossing put her safety in danger, and all because I couldn't keep a lid on my feelings for her.

Fuck. Why the hell had I caved?

"You got a second?"

I looked up from my desk and saw Mason standing in the doorway.

"What's up?" I asked.

He strode into my office and brandished his laptop, then slammed it down on my desk.

"I've got an I.D. on the bald guy from the store," he said.

"Fucking finally," I said, as I scooted his laptop towards me.

"I know it's been days, but it's a definite match. I ran it twice, just to be sure. It was difficult to find the son of a bitch, but we've got him."

Mason came around behind me and toggled through pictures he had pulled up. The bald man shaking someone's hand. That same man walking around the sidewalks of D.C. That same man purchasing a gun from someone he should have never been purchasing anything from. Then, Mason pulled up the security footage from the store, along with the facial recognition program software that had stopped on the man's identity.

"That's definitely our guy," I said.

"That's what I figured you would say, and that's not good," Mason said.

"Why not?"

"You don't recognize the name?"

My eyes scanned over the basic information of the man before my eyes bulged.

"Holy fuck," I said.

"Yep," Mason said.

"You've got to be kidding me."

"Not even a little bit."

"The mob? Are you kidding me!?"

I slammed away from my desk and quickly stood to my feet.

"To be precise, he's a lieutenant in a mob organization out of Philadelphia. Which also happens to be one of the three home bases for Senator Logan and Diana when they aren't in D.C. or at their vacation home in Alaska," Mason said.

I raked my hand through my hair before a growling sigh left my lips.

Wait, Alaska?

"Who the fuck has a vacation home in Alaska?" I asked.

"Beats me, but when I asked Senator Logan about it, that's how he described the house," Mason said.

"Did you tell him anything else?" I asked.

"No. I figured you wouldn't want me to. But, when I came across their financials and saw they had a home in Alaska, I asked him what it was for and he called it a vacation home."

"You know that's bullshit, right?"

"The stench was extravagant, Ethan."

"Okay. What do we know about Logan and Philadelphia?" I asked.

"Senator Logan's business interests are headquartered there. I've already looked into it. A few of his big-time donors as well as people he says he's trusted along the way in his career are all based out of that city. Plus, he's the damn senator of Pennsylvania."

"Shit. I forgot about that."

"Yep. Their roots run deep in Philadelphia. He campaigns there every year, whether it's a campaign year or not," Mason said.

"Okay. Here's what I want you to do. I want you to figure out exactly where that house in Alaska is. It's not a vacation home. That much I can tell you. I want the layout of the property, any bills attached to it and the names they're in. All of it."

"On it, boss."

"Until we know otherwise, we treat this as if Senator Logan has mob connections."

"You want me to inform Liam?"

"Yes. Go brief him on what you just told me and what we figured out. I have to place a phone call to the senator."

"I thought we weren't going to tell him about this," he said.

"We're not. But I do have a few questions for him and I want to know how he's going to answer them."

"Fair enough. I'll go find Liam."

"Thanks, Mase."

I watched my comrade walk out of the office before I picked up my cell phone. The mafia was targeting Senator Logan. Great. But why? Who the hell had he pissed off? I dialed Logan's cell phone and held it to my ear, but some idiotic assistant picked up and told me Congress was still in session and that he couldn't be reached. So, I left a message with the assistant Logan refused to give up and told her the damn thing was urgent.

I didn't even want to think about Senator Logan being tied up with the mob, but I couldn't shake all the evidence presented to me. Diana had accused her father of being tangled up in something he couldn't control. That someone was targeting them for a reason and that she deserved to know what it was. And Senator Logan was very quick to shut her up about the topic. Was it because he was connected to the mob? Was the reason for him keeping all of this so hush-hush the fact that he was entangled with an organization that could end his career in a flash?

It made me sick to think about.

Especially since Diana was a fruitful target.

The mob had no issues going after family members to prove points. So, if Logan had pissed someone off in their organization, it made sense as to why the threats were geared almost solely towards Diana. She'd be used as leverage before ultimately being killed.

Holy shit, there was a massive possibility that Senator Logan was connected to the mafia.

"Ethan?"

"Come in, Liam."

"I just talked to Mason."

"So, you're coming to see if what you heard was correct or if you stroked out for a second."

"Essentially, yes."

My eyes slowly gazed over to Liam and a groan left his lips.

"You've got to be kidding me," he said.

"I'm not," I said.

"The mob? Really?"

"That's what the evidence is pointing to right now. And the more you think about it, the more it makes sense. Why the senator wants to keep everything so quiet. Why he refuses to involve the police. Why Diana is being readily threatened as much as he is."

"So, what's our next move?" he asked.

"I'm bypassing Senator Logan with this decision, and I need you to shut your mouth on it."

"It's about damn time we stepped up and did that anyway. He can't keep running this investigation."

"I want you and Mason to take this information down to the Abingdon police department. I want them to know exactly what's going on, just in case the mob finds us here. Everywhere we go, the people around us are targets. And that includes the kind people in this very small town. This has officially careened out of control, and we need to make sure we keep as many people as safe as we all can in the process."

"The senator really isn't going to like that."

"Well, you know what I don't like? Politicians who get in bed with the mob and then expect people like us to bail them out," I said.

I drew in a deep breath before I closed my eyes.

"We're going to work with the police department in town to use the interstate database so we can collect any other information to use at our disposal. Tell them that they have our cooperation so long as we have theirs, and then let Mason sweet talk his way into their systems. We need to be prepared from all fronts, because this target isn't going to be easily eliminated. If we can get the Abingdon police force on our side, there's a very good chance we can get D.C. Metro to work with us as well. Which means we can track the senator without his knowledge and figure out what the fuck is going on."

"This isn't a target that you can eliminate at all, Ethan."

My eyes fluttered open and connected with my best friend.

"One step at a time," I said.

Liam nodded his head before he turned on his heels.

"One step at a time," I murmured to myself.

Chapter 22

Diana

E than and his crew of black-booted gunmen had been shut up in the office all damn day. Again. But, I wasn't going to let it get to me this time. Instead, I was going to make dinner for Ethan. Not all of the guys. Just him. They could eat Rebecca's casseroles. But I wanted to prepare something nicer for him. If I wanted to be with him, I needed to make myself a better catch. He obviously didn't prize looks over everything else, which meant I needed to show him the other tricks I had up my sleeve. Sure, I was smart and sexy as hell, but I wasn't really domestic. And the more I got to know Ethan, the more I understood that he wanted a woman that knew how to do more than call for carryout.

I could cook. It didn't look that hard. Just pick up some shit, throw it into a pan, and turn on the stove.

But, when I got into the kitchen to make dinner, I was lost.

There were spices and different kinds of noodles and four different types of butters. I needed extra virgin olive oil, not to be confused we regular olive oil—whatever the fuck that meant. There were different parts to a chicken, apparently. Thighs and breasts and legs. What was the part of the chicken I got when I simply ordered chicken? And what were all of these plug-in devices under the kitchen counter?

One looked like a torture device and the other looked like it was ready to mince my brain into shreds.

"Trying to cook something up?"

I turned my head at the sound of Man Bun's voice, watching as he leaned against the doorway with a grin on his face

"Could I ask you for a favor?"

"What's up?" he asked.

"Can I use your cell phone to call Miss Rebecca?"

I watched his brow tick in confusion before his eyes narrowed at me.

"It's not a trick. I have a craving for homemade noodles, but I'm a little lost on how to make them myself. I figured she might know how to walk me through the process."

"You want to cook," he said.

"You don't have to seem to shocked, asshole."

He chuckled and shook his head before he pulled out his phone. He dialed Rebecca's number before handing it over to me, then he rifled through the kitchen to get himself a snack. After a quick conversation and a slew of questions I wasn't comfortable answering, I got Ethan's mom to agree to come over and help me cook the meal I had in mind for Ethan and myself.

"Thanks," I said.

"Not a problem," Man Bun said, grinning.

I pulled out everything she told me to pull out while she headed over. Salt, pepper, flour, and eggs. I reached down below the kitchen counter and pulled out a device that looked like it could flatten a rock, and I heaved it onto the counter and plugged it in. According to Rebecca, this thing would help us flatten the dough-like stuff we'd make before cutting the noodles into strips. But all it looked like was a crank with two metal spindles that rubbed together, or something like that.

I'd never seen anything like it before.

"All right. I've got a nice cut of steak, some vegetables we're going to slice up, and some broth for us to use. I've got everything else here," Rebecca said.

I was so relieved to hear her voice.

"Thank you so much for coming over," I said.

"Of course, sweetheart. It's not a problem. It's been a long time since I've cooked in a kitchen with someone else. It'll be fun."

"Not with me. I just realized I have no idea what I'm doing."

"Doesn't mean you can't learn. Now come on, let me give you your first lesson in pasta-making."

I mimicked her movements, trying to match them exactly. I poured some flour into a mound in front of me before digging out a small hole and cracking my egg into it. And of course, the shell shattered and I had to dig out the remnants. Which meant flour blew everywhere with every flick of my finger. Which made me sneeze. Which blew the rest of my flour against the backsplash of the kitchen.

I heard Rebecca biting back a giggle as I groaned.

"It's okay. It takes practice. Come on. Make another mound, then crack the egg like this."

I watched her do it again, and after three tries I finally got the egg incorporated into the flour. She taught me how to roll it out before taking small chunks and rolling it through the torture device, and that was when the questions started to fly.

"So, is this dinner just for you?"

I grinned at her question as I cranked the device and spit out a flat piece of dough.

"It's for Ethan and I, actually," I said.

"You're cooking my son dinner?"

"Well, he's been holed up in that office all day, and he doesn't ever eat unless it's something quick. The man's practically been surviving off chips and reheated casserole for the past few days. And I figured it I was craving something different, then so was he."

"But not the rest of the men?" she asked.

"I'm pretty sure the rest of the men would rather shoot themselves then spend an evening eating dinner with me."

"I'm sure that's not true. What makes you think that?"

My eyes darted over to her before a grin slid across my cheeks.

"I see where Ethan gets his interrogation skills," I said.

"Well, a beautiful young woman wants my help to make my son dinner. Can't fault a mother for being curious."

"I figured he'd want something different, that's all."

"So, there's nothing going on between you and my son?"

I swallowed thickly as the two of us started cutting the dough into strips.

"Nope," I said.

"Dinner isn't for some special occasion?" she asked.

"Yep. He definitely gets his interrogation skills from you," I said, giggling.

"Well, either way? I'm sure my son will enjoy it. He's always been a sucker for a home-cooked meal."

Even more of a reason for me to learn.

"Okay. Now, once we get to this point, it's time to boil the water. Go ahead and grab that pot, put some water in it, and shake some olive oil onto the top of it until a nice sheen coats the top of the water."

"Extra virgin?" I asked.

"Always. Using any other olive oil is a no-no."

"Why is that?"

"Because it makes everything taste like shit."

I threw my head back and laughed as we began to boil the noodles, and before I knew it, they were done. They didn't take long to make at all, and we used the trial noodles to test out a few different sauces for the evening. Rebecca walked me through how to make three of them. A creamy alfredo sauce, a spicy Asian chili sauce, and a tomato-based marinara. I looked at the steak and the eggs, then took in all of the vegetables we still had yet to chop up.

"Why don't we make one of those yakisoba noodle bowls or something?" I asked.

"A what?" Rebecca asked.

"You know, one of those noodle bowls. It'll have noodles and a bit of broth. Some thinly-sliced vegetables with a nice spicy Asian sauce.

Then, there's a poached egg and meat placed on top, and it's this nice little meal in one bowl."

"That sounds fantastic. Ready to get started?"

"As ready as I'll ever be."

Making dinner with Ethan's mother was a trip, to say the least. I yelped when the steak caught on fire to burn off the alcohol Rebecca had tossed into the pan. I sneezed because I got too much pepper up my nose and it blew boiling water onto the backsplash. It took me six eggs just to get one poached egg right. So, ultimately, that one went into Ethan's bowl. I settled for a scrambled egg mixture in mine, because I didn't know how the fuck to replicate that damn thing again. And I cut myself twice trying to follow Rebecca's instructions on how to cut the damn vegetables.

But an hour and a half later, dinner was done and Rebecca was sneaking out the back door.

"Something smells good in here," Liam said.

I watched him poke his head around the corner before he darted his eyes around.

"I made dinner. A noodle bowl with steak, vegetables, and a nice broth," I said.

"Well, I wish we could stay for it. But the security guys are headed into town to talk with some people."

"Is Ethan going with you guys as well?"

"Nope. Someone has to stay behind with you and he volunteered. I hate that I'll be missing dinner. It smells fantastic."

"Thank you," I said, as I grinned proudly.

What Mr. Man Bun himself didn't know was that he had just handed me my perfect evening. Dinner alone with Ethan would turn out to be the best evening I could have wished for. Because I didn't even think about preparing dinner for any of the other guys. Which, in retrospect, would have looked very weird if Ethan was trying to keep things under wraps from them. I hardly figured a romantic dinner alone with him would constitute him hiding things from his staff.

Oh, well. Sometimes the best things in life worked themselves out naturally. And this night was turning out to be perfect.

I took the two bowls of food over to the table before rushing into the living room. I plucked a few candles off the mantle before rummaging around for a lighter, then proceeded to light them up. I poured each of us a glass of wine before I turned off the kitchen lights, then I opened the blinds behind the table to allow the first few shreds of moonlight trickle in through the glass.

I put the lighter away just as I heard footsteps falling against the floor, and suddenly my heart rate sped up. What if he didn't like the dinner? What if he was allergic to something? Nonsense. Rebecca would have told me if he was allergic to something. Would she have told me if he wouldn't like my dinner idea?

"What's all this?"

Ethan's voice ripped me from my trace as I stood next to the kitchen table.

"Surprise," I said.

His eyes narrowed at me before they fell to the candlelit dinner on top of the table.

"Well, aren't you going to say anything?" I asked.

"What's all this for?"

"I made us dinner."

"You what?"

"I made us dinner, Ethan."

His eyes rolled over my hands and I hid them at my sides. Had he seen the Band-Aids?

"You all right?" he asked.

"Of course. Why wouldn't I be?" I asked.

His eyes locked with mine and I felt my heart jump into my throat.

"Are you not hungry?" I asked.

"I didn't say that."

"Then why aren't you sitting down?"

"You haven't asked me to."

I snickered and shook my head as a nervous smile crossed my cheeks.

"Would you like to join me for dinner?" I asked.

But when I moved to pull out my chair, Ethan still didn't move. And I felt every single part of me go on high-alert.

Chapter 23

Ethan

The smells coming from the kitchen ripped me away from my paperwork. I knew the guys were about to head into town to speak with the police department, which meant I was to stay behind and watch over Diana. I preferred it that way, too. I wanted to make sure the very best looked after her, especially once night fell. And I knew there was no one would could protect her better than I could. Liam and Mason stuck their heads in and told me they were off, and that they were taking Granger along with them. I shooed them away so they didn't interrupt my train-of-thought with regard to the research I was doing, but the lovely smells coming from the kitchen grabbed my attention.

And it made me upset.

What the hell was my mother doing in the house? I didn't know what it would take to get her to stay away, but it was time to have a very serious conversation with her. I didn't care if I had to stick a fucking patrol officer with her that would arrest her if she even came near the property. Now that we were certain that the mob was involved, I'd stop at nothing to protect her. To shelter her from all this until the case was wrapped up and the threat had been annihilated.

But when I came out of the office and ventured into the kitchen, I didn't see what I expected to see.

"What's all this?" I asked.

Diana's eyes ripped up to mine as she stood beside a chair at the kitchen table. Candles flickered on the tabletop as soft moonlight streamed through the back windows. The protector in me wanted to rush over and close the blinds. To move Diana to a more secure location where she wasn't standing directly in front of a damn hazard point. But the decadent smells of the food on the table kept my attention trained on nothing but her.

"Surprise," she said.

I narrowed my eyes, trying to figure out what the hell was going on.

"Well, aren't you going to say anything?" Diana asked.

"What's all this for?" I asked.

"I made us dinner."

"You what?"

"I made us dinner, Ethan."

Diana cooked? I knew Diana. She didn't cook. My eyes slowly fell over her body before they came to her hands, and before she hid them at her sides I saw something akin to Band-Aids wrapped around her fingers. Was she okay? Had she hurt herself? Someone helped her cook. I knew that much for certain. But who in their right mind gave Diana a damn knife if they knew she wasn't a cook?

"You all right?" I asked.

"Of course. Why wouldn't I be?" Diana asked.

I locked my eyes with hers and watched her swallow deeply.

"Are you not hungry?" she asked.

"I didn't say that."

"Then why aren't you sitting down?"

"You haven't asked me to."

She giggled and shook her head, and I felt myself warming to the idea. Some planning had gone into this. The food. The candles. The preparation. The cooking. The mutilating of her fingers in order to get it done. I wasn't going to turn down a meal with her. Not by a longshot.

But, I wasn't going to let her off the hook, either.

"Would you like to join me for dinner?" Diana asked.

I watched her pull her chair out and sit down, but I still couldn't bring myself to move. But I was still incredibly confused as to why this was all happening. If someone had helped her cook, did they know about this dinner? About what it was for and the romantic atmosphere she'd set? Because if they did, that meant someone knew way too much about what was going on between us. Holy shit, had one of the guys helped her cook?

Too many questions surrounded this scenario, and I was starting to have a hard time making myself enjoy it.

"Aren't you going to sit?" she asked.

"Why did you cook dinner?" I asked.

"Because I wanted to thank you for everything you've been doing for me."

"So, you cooked dinner all by yourself."

She smiled and nodded her head, then I watched her shrug her shoulders.

"I might have had a little help learning a few things, but yes, I did make the food. Now will you sit down? You're making me nervous."

I finally forced myself to sit down and I watched Diana take a bite of her food. Everything seemed homemade. Right down to the damn noodles. Yes, Diana most certainly had help. But the pride in her eyes when she watched me take that first bite was unmistakable. No matter the help she had, she did make this dinner with her own two hands.

And it was fabulous.

"This is incredible, Diana."

"I'm glad you like it," she said, giggling.

"I didn't think you knew how to cook."

"I guess I've got my surprises, just like you do."

"What surprises?"

"This estate, for starters," she said.

Her eyes connected with mine and she offered me the sweetest smile I'd ever seen cross her cheeks.

"I didn't consider you at all domestic. Yet here you are, serving me a well-cooked and fully-balanced meal," I said.

She giggled and took another bite, slurping a noodle between those precious lips of hers. Every bite I took, I had to hold back a groan of satisfaction. Everything was in perfect balance in the bowl. The broth. The noodles. The meat and the vegetables. No one thing overpowered the other, and I found myself finishing it quicker than I would have liked. And between my full stomach, the two glasses of wine I had, and the moonlight that blanketed Diana's body, I was overcome with emotion I couldn't control. Everything about this was like a dream come true. A beautiful woman sitting in front of me with evidence of how hard she worked on this meal just to make sure I enjoyed it. Her smile was only for my enjoyment as she sat across the table with the candlelight flickering in her beautiful brown eyes.

Was it possible that I had been wrong about Diana?

"What are you thinking about?" she asked.

Her voice pulled me from my trance as I finished off the last of my wine.

"About you," I said.

"What about me?"

I thought about how she may not have been the spoiled brat I thought she was. I thought about how beautiful she was turning out to be. How self-possessed, strong and independent she was underneath the hurt she used as armor to close herself off to the world. I thought about the Band-Aids on her hands. How I wanted to kiss every hurt knuckle until they were healed. I thought about her legs wrapped around my body as I carried her up to her room, my lips unable to keep away from her skin.

I thought about how badly I wanted her. And how very alone we were in my childhood home.

"Just how surprised I am at this dinner," I said.

"Well, I'm really glad you like it. Honestly? It's the first time I've cooked anything like this for someone else. I'm happy it turned out well."

"Do you cook often?"

"Not really. I used to putz around in the kitchen with my mom. You know, until—"

I watched her eyes dance around the table before she took another bite of her food.

"After she passed, Dad hired a chef to help us out. He doesn't cook. Never has, never will. So, my expertise stops when the recipe does. And even then, sometimes I have to YouTube how to use a cooking implement before I can do anything."

I watched her take another sip of her broth as her face fell.

"I guess after admitting that, it isn't as impressive," she said breathlessly.

"You use the resources around you to fend for yourself, Diana. Everything about that is impressive," I said.

Then I just watched for a moment as a glimmer of happiness raked across her face before she slurped another noodle between those pouty lips of hers.

"Do you cook?" she asked.

"I get around. But for me, it's mostly throwing together ingredients that are already prepared. So nothing from scratch, like this."

"So you can tell it's from scratch?"

"Are you kidding? Oh, yes. There's always a massive difference in taste. Like I said, I'm very impressed."

"Well, you deserve a good meal after cooping yourself up in that office of yours all the time."

"I'm sorry if you've been feeling ignored again," I said.

"It's got nothing to do with that. I get that you're working."

I didn't even try to hide my confusion at her statement, and it caused her to laugh.

"Yes, I know I can be difficult. I know I don't make it easy on anyone. But that doesn't mean I'm stupid," she said.

"I didn't take you for stupid. Merely spoiled."

"Well, I can't fault you for that. I am spoiled. But, that spoiling took the place of having my father around after my mother died. He thought if he gave me things, it would make up for him never being around."

"That isn't how it works."

"Trust me, I know," she said.

"Have you ever talked with him about it?"

"Several times, actually. But he drones on about his career or re-election or Congress or paperwork. And I stop listening because it's the same excuse over and over again."

She picked up her bowl and slurped down the rest of her meal. A sound I found really entertaining as a small droplet trickled down her cheek.

"Oh my gosh," she said breathlessly.

I watched Diana pick up her napkin and quickly wipe at the trail of broth on her skin.

"That was very unladylike."

"Not to me," I said.

Our eyes connected and every part of me wanted to go over to her, take her in my arms, and press her against the window while kissing her.

"So, how was your day?" she asked.

I grinned at the question. So much domestication in the entire scene, and I found myself enjoying every second of it.

"Long. But over, thankfully. How was yours?"

"Interesting. I learned a lot of new things in the kitchen, some of them the hard way. I finally know how to cut vegetables the way I need to now," she said.

She held up her hand and I took in the Band-Aids.

"Are you all right?" I asked.

"Oh, yeah. They're fine. They only bled for a little bit."

"You bled, Diana?"

"Ethan, it was fine. I'm not very proficient with fresh vegetables. I'm like you. Or, was like you. I heated vegetables already sliced and diced. Par for the course, in my opinion."

"Can I see them?" I asked.

"They're fine, I promise. I could probably take these off now and they wouldn't even hurt."

"Do it, I want to see them."

"Ethan, it's not a big—"

But I shot her a look, and she finally complied. She stood up and walked over to me, then sat in a chair next to me and held out her hands. I slowly unwrapped her knuckles, taking in the skin she'd practically sheared off.

"Did you put any Neosporin on these?" I asked.

"They're just little cuts," she said.

I flicked my gaze up to hers and she sighed.

"No, I didn't."

"Sit right here. Let me get the first aid kit."

I picked up our dirty dishes and put them in the sink, then grabbed the kit from the top of the refrigerator. I sat back down and got to work, wiping at the wounds with alcohol pads. Diana hissed at the contact, jerking back as I held her hands steady. I placed a dollop of soothing salve on each of the cuts, then wrapped them in fresh Band-Aids. She physically injured herself cooking me dinner. A thought I still couldn't wrap my head around. Diana, the young woman who pitched a fit the first time I ever met her simply because I wouldn't let her stay at a party, and she had sacrificed her comfort to make me a meal.

"I'll go get the dishes into the dishwasher," she said.

Before I could stop her, she was out of her chair and making her way to the sink. I stood up and followed her in, then started gathering the dirty dishes off the stove and the counter. She ran some warm water and rinsed everything off, then she passed them to me and I stuck them in the dishwasher. And every time she handed me a dish, our fingers brushed together. Heat pooled in my groin. My veins pulsed to life. It was the simplest scene—cleaning up after dinner—and yet my heart enjoyed it thoroughly with her. The rhythmic clinking of dishes as I settled them into the dishwasher. The rushing of water over the ceramic. The brushing of Diana's fingertips against mine.

And all of it after sharing a nice meal together.

After I closed the dishwasher, I got it started while Diana rinsed out the sink. I could no longer help myself. I was weakened by her. My walls had eroded into dust by the tame, beautiful and peaceful evening we had just spent together. I stepped behind her and slid my arms around her waist, then pressed my lips against her neck. I heard her sigh as she melted into my arms, her head falling off to the side to give me more of her.

I nibbled at her skin as her ass ground into my cock.

Gripping her hips, I slowly turned her around as the water kept running behind her in the sink. I kissed up her cheek, moving my way slowly towards her lips. I felt her gasping. Heard her whimpering as her hips gyrated against mine. Her arms threaded around my neck as our foreheads connected, her breath coming in short pants against my lips.

I could no longer keep myself strong against her. I wanted her. No. I needed her. My heart beat for her. My soul longed for her. And after waking up next to her and feeling the pain it brought me to slip away from her soft grasp, I knew I could never go back. This woman—who was the exact opposite of everything I thought I knew about love—had somehow wiggled her way into my chest and taken up space in my heart.

Space I didn't think would ever be free to a woman. Especially one like her.

"Kiss me," Diana whispered.

I brushed my lips against hers as my leg pressed between her thighs.

"Please," she pleaded.

My eyes opened and caught her stare, and I saw her want. I felt her heat and I heard her desperation for me. So tonight, I wouldn't hold back. Tonight, I would give her everything. All of me. Every single part of me that I'd given away in high school. I'd show her exactly what she meant to me, and I wouldn't leave her with a single doubt in her mind.

Diana would know I had fallen for her by the end of this night.

Chapter 24

Diana

T he intensity of his gaze shot shivers up my spine. The way his lips pressed into my neck and the way my body caved to him swirled my mind in ways I'd never experienced before. I wanted this. I wanted it more than I could stand. And yet, I didn't want him to do it if he didn't mean it. I knew what being with him meant to me now. I was falling for him. Hard. And the idea that he could want me without feeling anything for me broke my heart. But the look in his eye painted another story. The grip of his hands whispered a different type of secret that echoed off the corners of my body. He didn't look at me with the gaze of a man drowning in lust.

He looked at me with the gaze of a man drowning in love.

"Kiss me," I whispered.

His lips brushed against mine and it took all I had to stay upright on my feet.

"Please," I begged.

His lips connected with mine in the softest, most sensual kiss I'd ever experienced. There was nothing heady or needy about it. Just a simple gesture shared between two people who enjoyed one another's company. His hands gripped my hips before sliding around to my back. His hands splayed along my spine, holding me close to him. My lips meshed with his. My tongue slid against the slit of his mouth. He parted his beautiful mouth to greet mine as our tongues collided, and it shot me into another realm. Another galaxy. Another dimension altogether. Fireworks burst in my mind and my legs caved, but instead of plummeting to the ground I felt him pull me closer into him.

I was overwhelmed by the sensuality of it all.

He hoisted me onto the kitchen counter, then slowly pressed my legs apart. He slid his strong body against my thighs and I felt heat pooling quicker than I could stand. I cupped his cheeks as I tilted my head off to the side, slowly deepening the kiss. He sucked on my lower lip. His fingertips danced along the exposed skin of my thighs. I whimpered against his mouth, feeling my lips swell with their constant contact against his body.

And still, he didn't let up.

His kisses took my breath away and his skin felt hot against mine. Fire shot through my veins as his arms cloaked my back. I wrapped my legs around his body. I threaded my arms tighter around his neck. I inched myself to the edge of the counter so I could press the whole of me into his body. I wanted to feel all of him. I wanted his muscles pressing into the excess of my form. My hands slid down his chest and tugged at his shirt, pulling it from beyond the belt of his black pants.

"Come with me," he murmured.

His hands fisted my ass and he picked me up effortlessly from the counter. I giggled as his face fell to my breasts, and I felt his lips pucker to kiss my skin. I smiled as I wrapped my arms around him. I clung to him as he made his way to the stairs. I sighed and inched my way down his body, then buried my face into the crook of his neck.

I knew where he was taking me.

And I couldn't wait to get there.

He slowly ushered us into his room and I shut the door behind us. He locked the door before he settled me down onto my feet, then his lips promptly found mine again. His hands cupped my cheeks. Cupped the back of my head. Ran through my hair and traced down my body. It was as if he wanted his hands everywhere, all at once. And it shivered me to my core. I slid his shirt over his head and allowed my fingertips to dance in the divots of his chiseled muscles. I kissed down his neck and he removed my clothes from me, tossing my shirt to the floor and peeling my bra from my bosom.

He slowly backed me to the bed, and when I collapsed onto the sheets, both of us were naked against the other.

His lips kissed down my pulse point as his hands traveled down the sides of my legs. But I didn't simply want to lay there for him. I wanted to taste him. Touch him. Command him in every way like he did me. I locked my legs around his body and flipped him over, giggling at the way he groaned in shock. I straddled his naked pelvis and ground my pussy against his cock. My folds encompassed him, coating him in my wetness as my lips fell to his neck. I nibbled on his skin. I bit into his shoulder. I wanted to mark him the way he had me so many times, but I only wanted him to know it was there. I pressed my lips against every muscle of his body I could reach. I slid down his form, lapping at the rings of his abs and threading our fingers together while his cock jumped for my viewing pleasure.

Then, I seated myself between his legs as my eyes fluttered back up to his.

"Ethan?" I asked.

His icy blue eyes grew dark with storm clouds of lust as I hovered my lips over his leaking dick.

"Yes?" he asked gruffly.

"Hang on for the ride," I said.

Then I gripped his hands, shuffled my shoulders underneath his meaty thighs, and dipped my lips over the head of his cock.

Chapter 25

Ethan

As her lips ran down around my cock, my entire body exploded with electricity. Fuck. Her plump lips wrapped around my base, taking all of me back as it slid down the crook of her neck. Diana gripped my hands. I threaded our fingers together and curled my toes. Her cheeks hollowed out, pulling precum from the tip of my dick as groans choked from my throat.

"Oh, fuck," I grunted.

She hummed with delight around my thick dick and my eyes rolled back into my head.

I knew I was falling for her. I'd never felt this way about a woman before. Even Layla, all the way back in high school. I was shocked to admit it even to myself, but I wanted Diana more than I'd ever wanted Layla. Her curves. Her sass. Her strength and her independence. I wanted everything about Diana, all the time. Next to me. Against my body. In my ear. And as Diana sucked my cock, I felt my heart soar for her.

I was falling for Diana Logan, and there was nothing I could do about it.

My hips rolled into her face. I felt my cock curve down the back of her throat while her lips swelled around my girth. I felt my balls pulling up. I felt that telltale burn trickling behind my abs. I didn't want it to end. Not now. Not down her throat like some common cocksucker. I wanted to be inside of her. Close to her. Connected with her when my dick unleashed.

I managed to work my hand from the entanglement of hers before I fisted her hair and pulled her off my cock.

"No, no, no. You were so close," she whispered.

I pulled her body up mine and pressed our lips together, feeling the way her soft curves coated my body.

"That's not how I want you tonight, Diana."

My hands slid down her body and fisted her hips, guiding her pussy folds over the ridges of my thick cock.

"This is how I want you," I whispered.

Our eyes connected and I watched her beautiful amber gaze reflect the starlight dripping through the window of my room. She rocked her hips back and forth, slathering my cock in her juices. Her warmth shook me to my core. Her hands curled into my chest as she rose up. Her raven hair fell around her face, cutting us off from the rest of the world as I guided her hips up. My cock stood at attention for her. It leaked from her valiant efforts as her swollen pussy caught the tip of my dick. And when I sank her down my shaft, the way she shook for me filled me with a pride I'd always succumb to.

I'd always be weak for her. And I accepted my fate.

"Ethan. Holy hell."

"Follow my lead, Diana. Relax."

I guided her hips, swiveling and rolling as my dick swelled against her falls. She shivered as her toes curled, her hips bucking against mine. She looked so beautiful on top of my body. Full of my cock and dripping her fluids down my balls. I dug my heels into the mattress. I slowly coaxed her towards a faster pace. Her tits bounced for my viewing pleasure and I reached up for them, massaging them and tugging on them as she threw her head back.

"Oh, Ethan. I love your touch. The feel of you. Don't stop."

Her words shocked me to life and I rose up, wrapping my arms around her. I planted my face into her soft bosom before I flipped her over into her back. She squealed, and I covered her lips with mine. Silenced her sounds of joy as I drove into her body. Her legs wrapped around me. Her ankles locked as she bucked against my body. My hands found hers and our fingers threaded together, and soon I pinned them above her head. She opened up to me. Her juices coated my skin. My tongue raked over the roof of her mouth and traced the outlines of her teeth.

She whimpered down my throat. The softest sound that sent waves of goosebumps rushing down my form.

"Mhm. Mhm. Mhm. Mhm."

I suckled on her lower lip as her body began to quake. I felt her pussy rippling. Squeezing. Pulling me deeper as she approached her end. My eyes connected with hers and I watched her. I watched the way she kept her eyes on me, even when they wanted to flutter closed. I released her hands and cupped her cheek, propping myself up so I could keep my pace. Her arms raced around my neck, her face burying into the crook of it as she came unraveled against me.

"Oh, Ethan! I'm cumming! Yes! Don't stop!"

Her muffled voice against my skin forced me to stop. I slammed myself deep into her body as her juices sprayed from between her legs. She soaked me. Marked me as her own while I worked my arms around her back. I pulled her up from the bed, her weakened body close against mine as I sat back on my heels.

She was helpless to my assault as I continued thrusting up into her, my ass sitting back onto the mattress.

I held her close. I kissed her skin. I felt her rocking against me, even as her sweat dripped onto me. I curled my fingertips into the softness of her body as my legs locked up. My back rippled with heat as her nails dug into me. I growled into her shoulder. My lips found hers and I kissed her again. Her juices. Her smell. Her heat. Her sounds. It all swirled around my head in an endless pit of pleasure and darkness as my body finally let go.

Finally released.

Finally filled her the way I loved.

"Oh, yes. I'm cumming. Ethan. Fill me up. Please. Don't hold back on me. I can't take it."

My jaw quivered as her tits pressed into my chest. I peppered her skin with kisses as the two of us fell to the bed. My cock stayed buried in her, my hips slowly pumping us through our orgasms. I jolted. Jerked. Moved with her movements as she sought her end on the tip of my dick. Her jaw unhinged in silent pleasure and every inch of her body flushed with a healthy tint. I couldn't take my eyes off her. Even as we laid there, connected at the hips, I couldn't stop looking at her as the two of us fell asleep.

She curled naturally into my body as the two of us slipped off into a slumber, and for the first time in my life my body felt fulfilled. Satisfied.

Whole.

But before I knew it, my mind conjured a scene that looked all too familiar. I walked through the woods out back from my house until I was dumped into the garden. Wildflowers grew everywhere and the wind whipped harshly in the air. Off in the distance, the gazebo was seen. The stone glistened in the light of the sun and I saw a figure emerge from it. The shadowy shaped called to me. Waved at me to come on an adventure. I sprinted as hard as I could towards the person, ready to take Diana into my arms and pull her close.

However, when I got there, I didn't find Diana.

It was Layla.

I watched as her baby blue eyes filled with tears and her wispy blonde hair glistened in the sunlight. My jaw dropped open as my eyes gazed upon her form. Her grown, womanly form, with long legs and slim arms and the slightest hint of curves underneath her beautiful, silken summer dress.

My Layla.

"You remember when you first brought me here?" she asked.

My eyes fell to the gazebo and I saw an image of us as teenagers. My hands groping every part of her I could while her lips tentatively explored my neck. That same pit. That same gazebo. In that same garden where I'd brought Diana. It was the first time I'd ever fooled around with Layla. The first time my fingers had ever slipped into the warmth of a woman's body.

"Don't you remember?" Layla asked.

"I do. I'll always remember," I said.

"You didn't remember then."

I looked back over and saw an image of Diana and myself. My body scooting closer to hers. My lips caressing the shell of her ear. My hands eagerly picking her up and sitting her on my lap.

I had to look away. I couldn't bear watching it play out. I felt like an asshole. I looked into the baby blue eyes of the woman I had betrayed. The sweet, kind, innocent young girl whose life had been ripped from her all too soon. I watched a tear trickle down her cheek and I reached out to swipe it away. But before my thumb to fall onto the soft, creamy skin I missed so much, a familiar voice called out to me.

"Ethan! Come on!"

I whipped my head around and saw Diana waving at me from the other side of the lake.

"I'm talking to someone. Give me a second!" I exclaimed.

I watched Diana crook her finger at me as a grin crossed her cheeks.

"You're being silly, Ethan. There's no one else out here but the two of us," Diana said.

"No, really. Give me a second. I'm catching up—"

But when I turned my face back to take in Layla, she was gone. And the only thing left behind was her tear on the tip of my thumb.

I jerked myself awake from the dream, sweat pouring down the back of my neck. My muscles shivered in confusion as goosebumps trickled along my limbs. What the fuck kind of dream had that been? And yet, the guilt still hung heavily in my chest. I looked down at Diana next to me. The naked woman with sloping curves and olive skin and an attitude that was slowly beginning to shift. I reached out to run my hand along her back, but for some reason it felt wrong.

It felt wrong to touch her.

I slid from the bed, leaving Diana to sleep as nighttime still hung heavily in the sky. I walked into the bathroom and closed the door behind me, then quickly turned on the hot water. I needed to shake the cobwebs of that dream from my mind. I needed to right myself before a new day dawned. Because if there was anything that would derail me from protecting her, it was my guilt.

And I really hoped a hot ass shower would help.

Chapter 26

Diana

My eyes fluttered open the next morning and I already knew what had happened. The emptiness hung there, even though my body hadn't explored the bed yet. I braced myself for the disappointment. For the sadness I knew would overwhelm me. Then, I drew in a deep breath and moved my arm off my chest.

My hand fell to the empty side of the bed next to me and I felt sadness pool in my chest. Disappointment washed through my veins as I laid there, staring at the ceiling while my body ached in glorious pleasure. What the hell was it going to take to get Ethan in bed with me all night? Last night had been insane. It was intense, and erotic, and so romantic. It was the most romantic thing I'd ever experienced. I knew we shared something. I had no doubt in my mind about it any longer. But waking up in an empty bed constantly placed doubts in my mind.

Was it possible that Ethan wasn't staying with me because he didn't feel the same way I did?

I pulled myself out of bed and put my clothes back in. I waited until the hallway was quiet, then I slipped out and back into my room. I chucked my clothes into a corner and made my way for the bathroom, ready for a warm shower to slowly ease my aching muscles. Was it possible I had given my heart to the wrong guy?

Yeah, it was possible.

It had happened before. Twice, in fact. Well, I hadn't fully given my hart to either of them, but I had started the process. I tried trusting them and relying on them to see if they were worth their weight in salt. And both times, I got to a point where I saw myself falling in love with them. Having a future with them. Creating a life with them. Then, it bit me in the ass.

I was worried that Ethan and I would meet the same fate.

In some ways, I'd already fallen in love with him. I'd never felt this way about a man before. Sure, I'd indulged in my fair share of hookups. But serious boyfriends were few and far between, and both times I'd had them I didn't feel anywhere near this strongly. It worried me. As I washed my hair and allowed the warm water to ease the tension from my muscles, I wondered if I had made a mistake.

I wondered if Ethan still regarded me as a mistake.

It was hard not to think about it. After all, I'd slipped from the beds of many men. And there were two reasons why I did so. One, because I woke up and didn't want them to wake up and get the wrong impression about us; or two, because they were nothing but a hookup and I didn't want to be reminded of it any more than I had to be. One was based out of a fear that the guy would read more into it, and the other was based on my shame.

The idea of Ethan doing that to me made my heart hurt.

I stepped out of the shower and got myself ready for the day. Drying off, I slipped into some clothes, and decided to do my makeup and hair. Maybe I could catch his attention by being the beautiful woman I knew I was. I put on a pair of shorts that were a little too short for my father's liking, and curled my hair. I applied my crimson lips and cat-eye makeup, making sure to wear a pair of heels that really flexed my legs. A loose little shirt that fell off my shoulder along with a multicolored bra strap was sure to catch his eye.

I was in for another bucket of disappointment, though, once I made my way downstairs.

Ethan was already locked away in his office and annoyance filled my body. I knocked on the door and announced myself, but I didn't even here so much as an answer. Fine. If he really wanted to regard me as nothing more than something to be ashamed of, then I wasn't wasting any more time on him. I wasn't staying cooped up in the house with him, either.

A walk was in order. Yes, I wanted to take a walk. To get some fresh air and enjoy the world around me a little bit.

Changing out of my heels and into some flats, I made my way towards the backyard. I followed the same trail and found myself walking through the same secret garden he had showed me a week or so ago, and a smile crossed my cheeks. It really was beautiful out there. The small lake reflected the sky perfectly and the stone-foundation gazebo called to me again. I made my way over to the gazebo and walked inside, my eyes scanning the pillows and the glassless windows and the inlaid stone seats.

I felt a peace come over me. A calm unlike anything I'd ever experienced. And I wondered what it was from.

Sitting on the edge of the stone benches, I looked around the gazebo. And everywhere I looked, there was evidence of Ethan's childhood. I found more army men stuffed underneath the pillows and a couple of small hats shrouded in a shadowy corner. I slipped from the bench and knelt down, looking underneath the stone seating. I pulled out more army men and a couple of miniature toy guns. The smallest little boy hoodie I'd ever seen and one lonely sock. My smile grew as I discovered more and more of Ethan in this place. Little Ethan, baby boy, enjoying his secret world.

Then, my eyes scanned up the wall and I found a carving in the corner.

I got up and walked towards it, my fingers tracing over the tainted stone. The carving was shaky, at best. My fingernail ran along the letters as I drew in a deep breath, my eyes dancing over the heart shape that was filled with initials.

ES + LJ = 4-EVER

I knew 'ES' was Ethan Stark. That much was for certain. The mark of his childhood was all over this gazebo. But who was 'LJ'? And what happened to forever? It was obviously part of his past. And some-thing—or someone—that had meant a great deal to him. I couldn't stop tracing over the image. Over the heart. Over the initials. I couldn't stop feeling the energy that coursed up my arm as memories poured from the walls of the gazebo. Electricity shot up my arm in a flash and I pulled away, suddenly spooked by the memories that the walls had ab-sorbed.

It was time to be heading back anyway. For all I knew, Ethan had called the damn National Guard to find me by now.

If he even knew I was gone in the first place.

Back at the house, I heard Rebecca humming in the kitchen. Not a soul was to be found as I made my way in there, and it made me sigh. I guess Ethan hadn't realized I'd left after all. I saw her making sandwich-es and stacking them onto a plate, and when she heard me coming in she turned around and smiled at me.

"Hey there, Diana."

"Hey, Mrs. Stark."

"You can call me Rebecca, you know."

"What are you up to?" I asked.

"Just making some sandwiches for the guys."

"Need any help?"

"Actually, yes. I need the chips out of the pantry and the meat from the pull-out drawer in the fridge."

"I'm on it," I said.

This was my chance to get some information out of Ethan's mother about who 'LJ' might have been.

"So, what was Ethan like when he was younger?" I asked.

She cast me a side-glance before a grin spread across her cheeks.

"He was an adventurous little boy. Always playing with these little action figures and losing them all around the house. I stepped on more of them throughout the course of my life than anything else."

"I can't imagine that would've felt good," I said.

"It didn't. I've got plenty of scars on the bottoms of my feet to prove it."

"Ouch. Any stitches?"

"Many. But I never told him that. He was a sensitive boy, too. Always worried about me. So, I never gave him a reason to if I could help it," she said.

"What about school? Did he like school?"

"Loved it. Especially when it got into high school."

"Because of the girls?" I asked coyly.

And when Rebecca didn't respond, I looked over at her to see if she was okay. I watched her stare grow far-off. She sort of blanked out for a second before she shook her head and came back to reality. She handed me a piece of bread with mustard and mayonnaise on it, and I filled it with meat and cheese before grabbing another slice of bread and finishing off the sandwich.

"His favorite subject was science, believe it or not. I knew for a fact he was going to be a scientist one day, until he expressed interest in joining the military after getting a degree in absolutely nothing to do with the subject," she said.

"Doesn't sound like Ethan dated much," I said.

"Not since high school, no."

I eyed her carefully, waiting to see if she would offer up the information.

"Are you okay?" I asked.

"Yeah, yeah. It's just—"

I turned my body towards her, pausing the sandwich-making so I could look her in her eyes. There was so much pain and sorrow. Hurt and anguish. She dabbed at her eye before she placed her knife down, then she turned to me and sighed.

"Ethan's a good man. But, he's not without his faults. I know you're curious about him. I can tell. And I know he's curious about you, too," Rebecca said.

"I'm more concerned right now with the button I've obviously pressed. I'm sorry. I didn't mean to bring up such obviously painful memories," I said.

"High school was hard on Ethan. It was hard on all of us, really. He was a good boy, and found himself a sweet girl to spend his time with. But, life doesn't always go as planned, and she passed away at a very young age."

"Oh my gosh, I'm so sorry."

I reached my arms out for Rebecca and wrapped her up in a hug. I no longer cared about the initials. All I cared about was the woman in front of me that was obviously still grieving a loss Ethan experienced in high school.

Was that why he was always so closed-off? Because he still hurt, too?

"Do you want to talk about it?" I asked.

Rebecca sniffled and pulled away before she picked up a napkin and wiped at her eyes.

"Layla was a beautiful girl. Vibrant. Soft-spoken. Full of life. Ethan was hell-bent on marrying her. He came to us on the night of their senior prom and announced that once they graduated, he was going to ask her to marry him."

"Are you serious?" I asked.

"Yeah. He was head-over-heels with that girl, and it was obvious as to why. The two of them fit one another like a glove, you know? She was the sweetest girl we'd ever come across. Blue eyes. Blonde hair. She came from a good, strong family with good, strong morals. Those two could talk about anything, or nothing. The only trouble Ethan ever got into in high school was when we caught him sneaking out to go talk with her on her porch."

I felt my heart sink as my hand slid up and down Rebecca's arm. I tried to comfort her, but I couldn't help how my mind swirled. How my stomach sank. I was almost certain the 'L' in 'LJ' stood for 'Layla,' and the way Ethan's mother described her made her sound like a dream. Like the sweetest southern belle to ever exist. And learning that Ethan had every intention of marrying her answered so much.

It especially answered why he was ashamed of me.

I was nothing at all like her. I didn't look like her, or sound like her, or hold myself like her. If Ethan had a type, I was the complete opposite.

"Ethan changed after that. He ventured into this shell he never really came out of," Rebecca said.

"It looks like all of you guys suffered somewhat of the same fate with her death," I said.

"We never talked about it much. Not after the funeral. It made Ethan upset and I hated seeing him that way. But her death impacted all of us. The entire neighborhood. We all grew up together. I bought Girl Scout cookies from her as a little girl. I babysat her when her parents wanted to go on date nights. She and Ethan practically grew up together. And when she died, it felt like one of my own children died as well."

I wrapped my arms back around Rebecca, not knowing what else to do. But if Layla was the person behind the initials in the gazebo, it made sense. If Ethan took the 'forever' part seriously, there was a chance he was still in love with his high school sweetheart. The girl next door. The sweet, doe-eyed beauty his mother kept describing. I'd never be able to compete with something like that. I could never compare with the beauty of a soft, southern girl. I wrapped Rebecca up tight and let her release the emotions she'd held in for all these years, and I forced my mind to stop swirling. To stop analyzing. To stop dropping pieces into place.

But I couldn't help it. Her story answered so much.

And even though I tried to push past it, it had me worried. I couldn't compete with a ghost. Especially a perfect one. Maybe Ethan was ashamed of me. Ashamed of cheating on the one true love of his life, with the likes of me.

Fuck. I'd done it again.

I'd given my heart to the wrong man.

Chapter 27

Ethan

Slamming myself away from my desk, I shot up to my feet. Today had been utter shit, and my mood reflected that steaming pile of shit. Everything I'd learned about the Philadelphia mob was bad. Very, very bad. And every thread Mason dug up connected them more and more to Senator Logan. And Logan to them. And everyone else to everything else. I raked my hands through my hair and growled. As Mason connect more threads, it became clearer and clearer that the senator had gotten himself into this situation by trying to fuck over the damn mob. Was he insane?

Talk about a clusterfuck of nonsense.

On top of all that, I had this thing going on with Diana. The dream from last night. It all swirled around in my head and filled me with an anger and a guilt I couldn't shake. It was a recipe for disaster, so I sank myself into my work and didn't come up for air.

Until my work made me so damn pissed off.

I finally emerged from my office around one in the afternoon and headed for the kitchen. I needed to grab myself a quick bite to eat. The only thing I'd had that morning was an entire pot of coffee and a stick of chewing gum, and my stomach was rebelling. I walked into the kitchen and found Diana tucking a plate away in the refrigerator. Her eyes turned and met mine before she backtracked her movements, then held it out for me to survey.

"This one's for you. Are you hungry?" she asked.

I was shocked to find her standing there, much less putting food in the refrigerator for me. I eyed the plate and took in the sandwich, chips, and homemade potato salad. I wanted to reach for the plate. I wanted to take it back into my office and get back to work. But there was a look in Diana's eyes I didn't like and suddenly, I forgot all about my stomach.

"Are you okay?" I asked.

"Why wouldn't I be?"

There was a shadow looming over her features. A darkness I'd never seen before. And that darkness made me nervous. I shook my head at the plate of food and she placed it into the refrigerator, and I turned my back to leave. I couldn't unpack what was going on with her. I had too much on my plate already. I had the mob breathing down her father's neck, a looming issue with my relationship with Diana, and guilt that kept filling my stomach with memories of a time long past.

"Why don't you ever stay in bed?"

Diana's voice stopped me in my tracks before I turned around to face her.

"What?" I asked.

"Why don't you ever stay in bed with me?" she asked.

I shook my head at her before my eyes darted around the room.

"We have a professional relationship, remember?" I asked.

"Is that—the only relationship we have?"

Her voice was so small. It wasn't something I was used to with her. The shadow on her features grew darker, and I could've sworn she was sad about something. I drew in a deep breath. I looked around the kitchen one last time before I took a step towards her. I had no idea how to respond to her, but if we were going to have this conversation now, then it needed to be a quiet one.

Though I preferred it to be a nonexistent one.

At least until the case was over.

"Do you think a relationship between us could work?" Diana asked.

My eyes fell to her face and I found her staring at my chest. Gone was the confident woman who took what she wanted without rhyme or reason. And replacing her was a self-conscious woman whose mind I wished I could read. Honestly? I had no idea how to respond. I didn't want to hurt her, but I'd been asking myself that same question all fucking night. Would we work? Could we work? Was it possible for us to work? Things with Layla had been so easy. Effortless. I knew from the moment I met her that we were both meant to be. I knew she was my future wife. I knew she was the one woman on the face of this planet that had been made to fit me perfectly.

But with Diana, things were always so complicated. Our lives fought us every step of the way. Hell, she fought me every step of the way. Her attitudes grated on my nerves and sometimes, it only seemed that the pull between us was nothing but sexual. We had moments, like dinner the other night. Or our time in the gazebo. But I didn't have that same comfort and innate capacity to 'get it' the way I had with Layla.

All I had with Diana were doubts and questions that flooded my mind on a daily basis and a sexual urge I couldn't control around her. Which only left me with more questions.

"We were thrown together by circumstance, and emotions are running very high right now," I said.

"That's not what I asked," Diana said.

"We have very little in common, when you boil it down. I never saw myself ending up with a girl like you."

"What kind of girl am I, then?"

Her eyes finally fluttered up to mine and I bit back a groan. Shit. We were really about to have this conversation. She wasn't going to like what I had to say, but I wasn't one to lie. Especially to someone I cared about.

"You're a rich girl, Diana. And with that richness comes a lifestyle you're used to. You're used to having things your own way. You're used to getting what you want, and anyone who doesn't fall in line gets run over. It's not all your fault. Some of it is parenting. Your father using money to compensate for his absence. But as an adult, it's your decision on whether or not to change that. And from what I've seen, you'd rather ride the wave of someone else's credit cards and accomplishments than make your own."

"No, you pigeonholed me as a spoiled and selfish brat without getting to know me. And now, you refuse to see past that initial deduction of me, even though I've showed you other sides of my person."

"I can't help it if it's the face you show the most."

"It's not, and you know it. Sure, I like spending money on finer things. What woman doesn't?" she asked.

"I've known a woman or two that didn't give a damn about 'the finer things.' There is more to life than high-heeled shoes, fancy handbags, and expensive food."

"I'm not spoiled, Ethan. You just want to think I'm spoiled because you don't like the fact that you're attracted to someone like me."

"Fine. Going on my theory of being a brat and pitching fits? Take right now, for instance. You're not getting the response you want from me, so you're getting upset. Which would be fine if you presented logical arguments, but you're not. You're trying to talk me into a point of view that's yours, instead of trying to understand where I'm coming from so you can sympathize with me."

"I'm not going to sympathize with someone who thinks I'm spoiled! And I'm not a brat, Ethan."

"You are. You're a brat who tries to force people in line with what you want, and you run away even though everyone is working hard to keep you safe. You snuck out to the party after telling your father you'd stay put, and I had to drag you out to the car to get you home. You snuck away from my men in the shoe store because you didn't want to come here and we had to drop everything to look for you. You left this morning to go wherever it was you went without notifying anyone, and I was two minutes away from sending the damn cavalry out to look for you. You don't care about anyone but yourself. You don't care about those of us working hard to keep you alive. And you don't care about the repercussions of your actions. All you care about is the reward you reap."

I watched something pass over her features before they set themselves into stone again. I knew I was being harsh, but I couldn't contain myself any longer. If she really couldn't see the type of person she had turned into, then obviously someone needed to stop up and inform her. Maybe it was the emotion from my dream or my confusion over how I felt for Diana. Maybe, in the back of my mind, I hoped she would see the reality of her circumstance and grow up a little bit. But once my mouth started going, I couldn't stop it.

"You sneak out to party, you sneak out to shop, and you don't give a damn about anyone else but yourself. So you can say you're not spoiled all the way to the bank. But when it comes down to it, you survive off other people's banks. That's the kind of girl you are," I said.

"Then why have you been obsessing over me?" she asked.

I scowled at her before I let out a growling breath.

"I've been paid to 'obsess' over you, remember?"

Diana's face collapsed into hurt and the strong girl was gone once again. The brat receded and the courage melted and I felt her push past me. She charged out of the kitchen, her feet falling on the hardwood floors as she headed to wherever she'd go to have her tirade. Everything inside of me screamed to go after her. To run and catch her and take her into my arms. But instead, I ignored my instincts and returned to my office.

I even slammed the door behind me to try and relieve some of the pent-up frustration coursing through my veins.

Her bedroom door slammed as well and I fell into my chair. The conversation was less than ideal, and while it held truth, it didn't hold all of it. But I knew things between us couldn't progress. It was better to break it off now before we got in too deep. The truth of the matter was that I couldn't be together with Diana. There were too many obstacles between us. Setting aside the fact that she was a client, we were two completely different people. We came from different worlds and had different interests. We had different morals and values and different ways we lived our lives. Not to mention that she was a distraction I couldn't afford. Someone was going to get hurt if I continued to indulge in her body and her whims instead of keeping my mind focused on the case.

And with all the latest developments, I needed all the mental focus I could get.

Chapter 28

Diana

I slammed my bedroom door behind me and collapsed onto my bed. I cried for over an hour into my pillow, feeling my heart shatter into a million different pieces. No matter what I did, Ethan would only see me as a spoiled child. Nothing more, nothing less. I'd never be that sweet little southern belle girlfriend. I'd never be the doe-eyed beauty he wanted in his life. I'd never sell Girl Scout cookies or be close to his mother or grow up down the road from them. And I sure as hell would never be able to compete with the perfection of a ghost. Ethan was right about me. I was a shopaholic rich bitch who wasn't good enough for the Stark family.

That realization hurt worse than I could have ever imagined.

I'd thought that for once, I found someone who would put me first. Someone who would take my side and stick up for me and stand there, holding my hand while we walked through life. I thought I'd found the man for me. The man of my dreams that I could wake up to every morning, cuddle with, and kiss. But he said so himself. He'd only been doing what he was doing because he'd been paid to do it. And hey, a hookup was a hookup, right? Why not dabble in the perks of my selfish ways while pulling a paycheck at the same time? It was fine to fuck the rich bitch. But he couldn't bring her home to his mommy.

The more I cried, the more my anger mounted. It built and it built until I could no longer contain it. Fine. If that was how Ethan felt, then it was on to the next man. Fuck him and his bullshit. I didn't have to take that from him. I didn't have to take it from anyone. Not my boyfriends. Not my hookups. Not my father. No one. I had plenty of men hitting me up on a regular basis that I could spend my time with.

Men that wanted to pour their money and attention over me so they could get me in bed. If I was going to be nothing but a fuck-toy, the least I could do was get something out of it besides a broken heart.

I pushed myself off my bed and strode over to my closet. I didn't have to do anything that asshole asked of me. Nor did I have to stay cooped up with him in this fucking home. I pulled out my suitcase and slammed it onto my bed, then started pulling out my clothes. I rolled them up and jammed them in, then pulled things from their hangers. If Ethan thought I was nothing but a runaway, then the least I could do was rise to his expectation. If Ethan thought I was nothing but a spoiled rotten child, the least I could do was make him proud in his assumption. It wasn't as if I was going to change it. I wasn't going to blink my eyes and turn into some prim and proper little girl for him to take as his little wifey.

Looking up, I caught a look at myself in the dresser mirror before I wiped away my tears.

He didn't deserve them. He deserved nothing else from me. He had his chance, and he blew it. I pulled out all the stops, too. Entertaining him on his trip into town. Listening to his childhood stories. Waking up in an empty bed hoping he'd eventually stay even one night. Hell, I even asked his mother to help me cook that selfish bastard dinner. His mother! The same woman he would never introduce me to as his girl-friend.

I slowed down the folding of my clothes before I brushed another tear away.

Fear slowly began to replace the anger. And the dose of fear was sobering. The threat against my family still existed. It was out there, looming and prevalent. But, they hadn't found me out here in the middle of Hell itself. Which meant I could keep hiding and not be found, so long as I stayed away from my cell phone and credit cards. I could stay hidden from those who wanted to kill my father, and from Ethan himself.

Which sounded like a good deal to me.

The only reason I was in this situation was because my father had been selfish. In his career and in his deals. He'd pissed someone off for the sake political gain, I was sure of it. None of this had anything to do with me. My father had done all of this on his own without considering the consequences his actions could have on me. Again. I didn't need to fill my life with him any longer. Ethan had turned out to be the same way, and I couldn't believe I fell for it. He took what part of me he wanted, left me alone in bed, and had not a care in the world about how his actions affected me.

Never again.

I'd never let myself fall into that trap ever again.

My hands shook as I zipped up my suitcase. I knew I was reacting out of pain. Hurt. Betrayal. Ethan had taken my heart and smashed it underneath the heel of his boot, and now my soul cried out for vengeance. But I wouldn't give it to him. I wouldn't give him the satisfaction of watching me lash out again. Maybe he liked it, or maybe it really did grate on his nerves. Maybe he sickly got off on it somehow before turning his sights to more innocent prey. None of it mattered now. Not a damn bit of it. Because I wasn't going to stick around this mansion and risk falling back into his arms, only to be hurt by him again.

I wasn't going to stay in this house and beg for his attention. I wasn't going to try and seduce him into bed again, thinking that all would be well if I simply held him close enough. I wasn't going to allow my desperate feelings to turn me into some begging, cheap little girl who hung off his pant leg and proclaimed she'd do anything for his attention. I was better than that. Stronger than that. More independent than that.

And if that was what he wanted from me, then he was about to get a cold dose of reality dumped over his head.

Ethan was a lost cause and I needed to give him up. I needed to wash my hands of him instead of foolishly convincing myself I could win him over. I wouldn't give up my dignity for any man, much less a man like Ethan. A man who played me for a fool, incited a game of tug-of-war, then walked away like he was somehow the victor in all of it.

I needed to get the fuck out of that house.

Packing up my toiletries, I stuffed everything under my bed, then I made my way into the kitchen. I hung around there for a little bit, hoping to catch Liam again. That tall, lean little thing was always digging around in the kitchen for snacks. Which meant I'd catch him eventually. I had my plan all laid out in my head. It would work beautifully, too. Because the last one did as well. The issue with the last time was that I had done it just to get Ethan's attention. To get him to chase after me in a selfish attempt to convince myself that he really, truly cared.

Maybe Ethan was right about me. Maybe I only did things for attention. But this time, it wouldn't be for attention. It would be to start a new life. To pave a new path for myself. To finally use my degree to make my own money and show the world that no matter what people thought of someone, they really could rise to great heights.

A life I could be proud of. A life without hurt and men and lies and deceit. A life without heartbreak and meaningless one-night stands and men who only hit me up when their cocks were cold.

That was the kind of life I wanted.

And it was the kind of life I'd create for myself.

"Do we have anymore of those chips from lunch?"

I grinned at the sound of Man Bun's voice.

"We do. They're in the pantry," I said.

"Thanks. Figured I'd get me a little snack before dinner," he said.

"That's fine. I'm sure no one will mind."

"Want some?"

"No, but thank you for asking."

"Anytime."

"Hey, Liam?"

I watched him toss some chips into his mouth as he turned to face me.

"Could I ask you for a favor again?"

"Want to call Rebecca?" he asked, grinning.

"Yeah. I figured maybe she could come over and hang out or something. It's boring, hanging around with guys who keep themselves shoved in an office, or just walking around the property."

"Trust me, I'm one of them and I think they're boring. Let me give her a call for you."

"Thanks, I really appreciate it," I said, smiling.

His eyes dropped down my body before he pulled out his phone, but he struggled to push the buttons with his greasy fingers. He grunted in frustration and I bit back a smile, sinking my teeth into my cheek. Finally, he tossed me the phone and I caught it in midair, then grabbed a napkin to wipe it off.

"Just put it on the kitchen table when you're done. I'll be back in a few," Liam said.

"Sounds good. And I'll make sure I don't get it coated in chip grease."

"Appreciate it!"

I waited until his steps receded, then I searched the name of the nearest taxi company. I held the phone to my ear as I walked towards the hallway, keeping an eye out to make sure no one was coming. The phone rang in my ear and I braced myself to talk as if I was speaking with Rebecca. But, when the line picked up and I found myself still alone, I cleared my throat and started in on my plan.

"Virginia Cab Company, where no part of the state is too remote for us. This is Cindy. How can I help you?"

"Hi there. I was wondering if I could arrange a taxi ride for early morning hours. I've got a flight out of Virginia Highlands at, like, five in the morning."

"Of course, ma'am. All we need is an address."

"Is it possible for you guys to stop at the end of the driveway as well? I don't want the lights of the taxi waking up the whole house. The front of it is littered with windows and I don't want to be rude," I said.

"We can pull up without our lights on, if you'd like."

"That would be perfect thank you so much."

"Two o'clock in the morning, this coming morning?"

"Yes, ma'am. As in, ten hours from now."

"Wonderful. All we need is an address and we'll be there," she said.

I rattled off an address I'd found on a piece of old mail stuffed in one of the kitchen drawers. Then I quickly hung up the phone. I erased the call from the call log and cleared Liam's search history on his phone, then dialed Rebecca quickly to make sure a call from her appeared in his phone. Thankfully, she didn't pick up. I wasn't sure about what I would say to her if she had.

"Any luck?" Liam asked.

I whipped around, trying my best to calm my fluttering heart as I smiled at Mr. Man Bun.

"Nope. She didn't pick up. But thanks for letting me use it," I said.

I tossed his phone back to him and watched him tuck it away in his pocket without even checking it. Part of me felt guilty for the fa-cade. In a way, I knew I was playing right into Ethan's assumption of me. But I couldn't bother myself with that. My life wasn't here, in Abing-don. Nor was it in D.C., with my absent father. It was somewhere else. Somewhere secluded and private, where people cared and families took care of their own and neighbors were friendly instead of back-stabbing bitches who wanted nothing more than fame or fortune at anyone's ex-pense.

After one last look around the kitchen, I finally found a sheet of pa-per and a pen, then I made my way back up to my bedroom.

The least I could do was leave him a note. A letter, describing why I was making this choice. If I didn't, he'd slam me for being selfish and running again. And even though I shouldn't have given a damn about what he thought of me, part of me still did. Part of me always would. I hoped that faded with time. With healing. I hoped I'd one day be able to shake the massive security guard from my mind and my heart.

But I knew it would take a while.

Ethan,

I know you'll think this is some ploy to get your attention, but it's not. Believe it or not, you are not as important as you think you are. So, if you are paid to come after me, don't bother. I'm safe, and I can look after myself. Contrary to what you or my father or anyone else thinks of me, I'm capable of leading my own life.

Do I want to live my life with someone? Of course. Everyone does. No one wants to be alone their entire life. But my father replaced himself with a credit card after my mother died, and all I had to get his attention with was my attitudes. Hey, at least my father was talking to me if he was yelling at me, right? But, I did lose myself in all of that. I did become a spoiled brat, but that's not who I am. At least, it's not who I want to be.

Don't look for me. I mean it. I don't want to see you and I don't want to hear from you. None of you. Not even my father. I'm a grown woman with a college degree, and I can take care of myself. None of you believe that, but simply having a belief doesn't make something true. Good luck with everything, and let my father know his credit cards will be abandoned.

—Diana

I folded it up and placed it on my pillow. I knew he'd ignore it, but at least I did my best. Just like I'd do my best to not be found this time. I ignored his calls for dinner and snickered when he didn't even come up the steps to look for me. Great. He was fine peeking in on me when I was masturbating in the damn tub, but if he knew he wasn't going to see me with my legs spread open he didn't even bother knocking on my damn door.

Typical male.

I stayed up late. I turned the light off in my room and gathered up my things. I listened as everyone slowly made their way to their rooms, Ethan included. I heard him take a shower. I heard him talking to himself. I heard him slam down into his bed and groan. Then, the house fell silent. Nothing but the sounds of crickets and rushing wind could be heard as the clock slowly approached two in the morning.

And at five minutes until two, I slowly crept out of my room.

Slinging my purse over my shoulder, I raised my suitcase over my head and hung my toiletry bag around my neck. I didn't want to make a sound. I timed my breaths with my steps, keeping myself as silent as I could. After walking out the front door, I slowly eased it shut behind me, listening to the lock click into place. I shuffled myself down the porch steps and made my way to the driveway, then ran as quickly as I could to the main road.

It was dark. Pitch black, in fact. The only reason I knew I was headed in the right direction was because of the sound of the concrete beneath my running feet. And when the house was nothing but an imprint on the hillside, I set my bag down and waited. Steeling myself against the taxi that would be pulling up at any moment.

And when it did, I felt a sigh of relief course through my body.

The taxi pulled up with its lights off and I ripped open the door. I shoved my things into the backseat before I slid in, closing the door beside me. I looked up at the shadowed mansion one last time, bracing myself for the end of an era.

"Goodbye, Ethan," I said to myself.

And this time, it was goodbye for good.

THE END

Her Champion – Book 3

When retired Special Forces military man Ethan Stark began his security firm, never in his life did he except to break his own rules.

He has three of them: Never get personally involved, never get blindsided, and never screw around. Ever.

But when Senator Chester Logan approaches him and uses his personal ties to cash in a favor, Stark feels compelled to accept. What he didn't expect was to have his nerves grated on by his only daughter, Diana. Nor did he expect his heart to break free from the shackles that guarded his darkest memory.

Protecting Diana Series

Her Bodyguard – Book 1
Her Defender – Book 2
Her Champion – Book 3
Book 4 – coming soon!
Book 5 – coming soon!

Find Lexy Timms:

LEXY TIMMS NEWSLETTER:
http://eepurl.com/9i0vD
Lexy Timms Facebook Page:
https://www.facebook.com/SavingForever
Lexy Timms Website:
http://www.lexytimms.com

Want

FREE READS?

Sign up for Lexy Timms' newsletter
And she'll send you updates on new releases,
ARC copies of books and a whole lotta fun!

Sign up for news and updates!
http://eepurl.com/9i0vD

More by Lexy Timms:

FROM BEST SELLING AUTHOR, Lexy Timms, comes a billionaire romance that'll make you swoon and fall in love all over again.

Jamie Connors has given up on men. Despite being smart, pretty, and just slightly overweight, she's a magnet for the kind of guys that don't stay around.

Her sister's wedding is at the foreground of the family's attention. Jamie would be find with it if her sister wasn't pressuring her to lose weight so she'll fit in the maid of honor dress, her mother would get off her case and her ex-boyfriend wasn't about to become her brother-in-law.

Determined to step out on her own, she accepts a PA position from billionaire Alex Reid. The job includes an apartment on his property and gets her out of living in her parent's basement.

Jamie has to balance her life and somehow figure out how to manage her billionaire boss, without falling in love with him.

** The Boss is book 1 in the Managing the Bosses series. All your questions won't be answered in the first book. It may end on a cliff hanger.

For mature audiences only. There are adult situations, but this is a love story, NOT erotica.

FRAGILE TOUCH

"HIS BODY IS PERFECT. He's got this face that isn't just heart-melting but actually kind of exotic..."

Lillian Warren's life is just how she's designed it. She has a high-paying job working with celebrities and the elite, teaching them how to better organize their lives. She's on her own, the days quiet, but she likes it that way. Especially since she's still figuring out how to live with her recent diagnosis of Crohn's disease. Her cats keep her company, and she's not the least bit lonely.

Fun-loving personal trainer, Cayden, thinks his neighbor is a killjoy. He's only seen her a few times, and the woman looks like she needs a drink or three. He knows how to party and decides to invite her to over—if he can find her. What better way to impress her than take care of her overgrown yard? She proceeds to thank him by throwing up in his painstakingly-trimmed-to-perfection bushes.

Something about the fragile, mysterious woman captivates him.

Something about this rough-on-the-outside bear of a man attracts Lily, despite her heart warning her to tread carefully.

Faking It Description:

HE GROANED. THIS WAS torture. Being trapped in a room with a beautiful woman was just about every man's fantasy, but he had to remember that this was just pretend.

Allyson Smith has crushed on her boss for years, but never dared to make a move. When she finds herself without a date to her brother's upcoming wedding, Allyson tells her family one innocent white lie: that she's been dating her boss. Unfortunately, her boss discovers her lie, and insists on posing as her boyfriend to escort her to the wedding.

Playboy billionaire Dane Prescott always has a new heiress on his arm, but he can't get his assistant Allyson out of his head. He's fought his attraction to her, until he gets caught up in her scheme of a fake relationship.

One passionate weekend with the boss has Allyson Smith questioning everything she believes in. Falling for a wealthy playboy like Dane is against the rules, but if she's just faking it what's the harm?

Capturing Her Beauty

KAYLA REID HAS ALWAYS been into fashion and everything to do with it. Growing up wasn't easy for her. A bigger girl trying to squeeze into the fashion world is like trying to suck an entire gelatin mold through a straw; possible, but difficult.

She found herself an open door as a designer and jumped right in. Her designs always made the models smile. The colors, the fabrics, the styles. Never once did she dream of being on the other side of the lens. She got to watch her clothing strut around on others and that was good enough.

But who says you can't have a little fun when you're off the clock?

Sometimes trying on the latest fashions is just as good as making them. Kayla's hours in front of the mirror were a guilty pleasure.

A chance meeting with one of the company photographers may turn into more than just an impromptu photo shoot.

Hot n' Handsome, Rich & Single... how far are you willing to go?
MEET ALEX REID, CEO of Reid Enterprise. Billionaire extra ordinaire, chiseled to perfection, panty-melter and currently single.

Learn about Alex Reid before he began Managing the Bosses. Alex Reid sits down for an interview with R&S.

His life style is like his handsome looks: hard, fast, breath-taking and out to play ball. He's risky, charming and determined.

How close to the edge is Alex willing to go? Will he stop at nothing to get what he wants?

Alex Reid is book 1 in the R&S Rich and Single Series. Fall in love with these hot and steamy men; all single, successful, and searching for love.

Book One is FREE!
SOMETIMES THE HEART needs a different kind of saving... find out if Charity Thompson will find a way of saving forever in this hospital setting Best-Selling Romance by Lexy Timms

Charity Thompson wants to save the world, one hospital at a time. Instead of finishing med school to become a doctor, she chooses a different path and raises money for hospitals – new wings, equipment, whatever they need. Except there is one hospital she would be happy to never set foot in again—her fathers. So of course he hires her to create a gala for his sixty-fifth birthday. Charity can't say no. Now she is working in the one place she doesn't want to be. Except she's attracted to Dr. Elijah Bennet, the handsome playboy chief.

Will she ever prove to her father that's she's more than a med school dropout? Or will her attraction to Elijah keep her from repairing the one thing she desperately wants to fix?

HEART OF THE BATTLE Series

In a world plagued with darkness, she would be his salvation.

No one gave Erik a choice as to whether he would fight or not. Duty to the crown belonged to him, his father's legacy remaining beyond the grave.

Taken by the beauty of the countryside surrounding her, Linzi would do anything to protect her father's land. Britain is under attack and Scotland is next. At a time she should be focused on suitors, the men of her country have gone to war and she's left to stand alone.

Love will become available, but will passion at the touch of the enemy unravel her strong hold first?

THE RECRUITING TRIP

Aspiring college athlete Aileen Nessa is finding the recruiting process beyond daunting. Being ranked #10 in the world for the 100m hurdles at the age of eighteen is not a fluke, even though she believes that one race, where everything clinked magically together, might be. American universities don't seem to think so. Letters are pouring in from all over the country.

As she faces the challenge of differentiating between a college's genuine commitment to her or just empty promises from talent-seeking coaches, Aileen heads to the University of Gatica, a Division One school, on a recruiting trip. Her best friend dares who to go just to see the cute guys on the school's brochure.

The university's athletic program boasts one of the top hurdlers in the country. Tyler Jensen is the school's NCAA champion in the hurdles and Jim Thorpe recipient for top defensive back in football. His incredible blue-green eyes, confident smile and rock hard six pack abs mess with Aileen's concentration.

His offer to take her under his wing, should she choose to come to Gatica, is a temping proposition that has her wondering if she might be with an angel or making a deal with the devil himself.

THE ONE YOU CAN'T FORGET

Emily Rose Dougherty is a good Catholic girl from mythical Walkerville, CT. She had somehow managed to get herself into a heap trouble with the law, all because an ex-boyfriend has decided to make things difficult.

Luke "Spade" Wade owns a Motorcycle repair shop and is the Road Captain for Hades' Spawn MC. He's shocked when he reads in the paper that his old high school flame has been arrested. She's always been the one he couldn't forget.

Will destiny let them find each other again? Or what happens in the past, best left for the history books?

** *This is book 1 of the Hades' Spawn MC Series. All your questions may not be answered in the first book.*

Did you love *Her Defender*? Then you should read *About Love* by Lexy Timms!

USA Today Bestselling Author, Lexy Timms, brings you a new series About Love and everything in between the road to forever.The course of true love never did run smooth... William ShakespeareAfter losing her money and fiancé in one go, Kellie Margolis, the one-time owner of a lucrative business, checks out of society. She needs to become something—or someone—unassuming. She's hired on as a waitress at a bar called Darkness. It's in a dangerous part of town, locally known for its Russian-American population.Betrayed and humiliated by her fiancé who used her business as a front for an escort service, Kellie wants to keep her world small and simple. Unexpectedly, her new life involves the erotic, shady, and incredibly charming Sasha Petrov. Sasha's too good-looking for words. Life for Kellie becomes passionate, adventurous, erotic, and bold—but by no means simple.Though too many signals say Sasha plays dirty, Kellie decides she'd be a fool to deny herself the pleasure he brings her. Their affair becomes more like a fairy tale, and Kellie starts believing Sasha is the love she deserves after her hard times. He lavishes her with opulence and tends to her every need like no one has ever done. When Kellie's past unexpectedly comes full circle, she realizes how small the world really is.Will an unforeseen discovery break Kellie's heart for good, or will Sasha be the bad boy hero he's set himself up to be?Just About Series:About LoveAbout TruthAbout Forever

Also by Lexy Timms

A Chance at Forever Series
Forever Perfect
Forever Desired
Forever Together

BBW Romance Series
Capturing Her Beauty
Pursuing Her Dreams
Tracing Her Curves

Beating the Biker Series
Making Her His
Making the Break
Making of Them

Billionaire Banker Series
Banking on Him

Billionaire Holiday Romance Series
Driving Home for Christmas
The Valentine Getaway
Cruising Love

Billionaire in Disguise Series
Facade
Illusion
Charade

Billionaire Secrets Series
The Secret
Freedom
Courage
Trust
Impulse
Billionaire Secrets Box Set Books #1-3

Building Billions
Building Billions - Part 1
Building Billions - Part 2
Building Billions - Part 3

Conquering Warrior Series

Ruthless

Diamond in the Rough Anthology
Billionaire Rock
Billionaire Rock - part 2

Dominating PA Series
Her Personal Assistant - Part 1
Her Personal Assistant Box Set

Fake Billionaire Series
Faking It
Temporary CEO
Caught in the Act
Never Tell A Lie
Fake Christmas

Firehouse Romance Series
Caught in Flames
Burning With Desire
Craving the Heat
Firehouse Romance Complete Collection

For His Pleasure

Elizabeth
Georgia
Madison

Fortune Riders MC Series
Billionaire Biker
Billionaire Ransom
Billionaire Misery

Fragile Series
Fragile Touch
Fragile Kiss
Fragile Love

Hades' Spawn Motorcycle Club
One You Can't Forget
One That Got Away
One That Came Back
One You Never Leave
One Christmas Night
Hades' Spawn MC Complete Series

Hard Rocked Series
Rhyme
Harmony

Heart of Stone Series
The Protector
The Guardian
The Warrior

Heart of the Battle Series
Celtic Viking
Celtic Rune
Celtic Mann
Heart of the Battle Series Box Set

Heistdom Series
Master Thief
Goldmine
Diamond Heist
Smile For Me

Just About Series
About Love
About Truth
About Forever

Justice Series
Seeking Justice

Finding Justice
Chasing Justice
Pursuing Justice
Justice - Complete Series

Love You Series
Love Life
Need Love
My Love

Managing the Bosses Series
The Boss
The Boss Too
Who's the Boss Now
Love the Boss
I Do the Boss
Wife to the Boss
Employed by the Boss
Brother to the Boss
Senior Advisor to the Boss
Forever the Boss
Christmas With the Boss
Gift for the Boss - Novella 3.5

Model Mayhem Series
Shameless
Modesty

Moment in Time
Highlander's Bride
Victorian Bride
Modern Day Bride
A Royal Bride
Forever the Bride

Outside the Octagon
Submit

Protecting Diana Series
Her Bodyguard
Her Defender

Reverse Harem Series
Primals
Archaic
Unitary

RIP Series
Track the Ripper
Hunt the Ripper
Pursue the Ripper

Tattooist Series
Confession of a Tattooist
Surrender of a Tattooist
Heart of a Tattooist
Hopes & Dreams of a Tattooist

Tennessee Romance
Whisky Lullaby
Whisky Melody
Whisky Harmony

The Bad Boy Alpha Club
Battle Lines - Part 1
Battle Lines

The Brush Of Love Series
Every Night
Every Day
Every Time
Every Way
Every Touch

The Debt
The Debt: Part 1 - Damn Horse

The Debt: Complete Collection

The University of Gatica Series
The Recruiting Trip
Faster
Higher
Stronger
Dominate
No Rush
University of Gatica - The Complete Series

T.N.T. Series
Troubled Nate Thomas - Part 1
Troubled Nate Thomas - Part 2
Troubled Nate Thomas - Part 3

Undercover Series
Perfect For Me
Perfect For You
Perfect For Us

Unknown Identity Series
Unknown
Unpublished
Unexposed
Unsure

Unwritten
Unknown Identity Box Set: Books #1-3

Unlucky Series
Unlucky in Love
UnWanted
UnLoved Forever

Wet & Wild Series
Stormy Love
Savage Love
Secure Love

Worth It Series
Worth Billions
Worth Every Cent
Worth More Than Money

Standalone
Wash
Loving Charity
Summer Lovin'
Love & College
Billionaire Heart
First Love
Frisky and Fun Romance Box Collection

Managing the Bosses Box Set #1-3